Careers
for the
Twenty-First
Century

Emergency
Response

By Tamara Thompson

LUCENT BOOKS

An imprint of Thomson Gale, a part of The Thomson Corporation

THOMSON

™

GALE

Detroit • New York • San Francisco • San Diego • New Haven, Conn.
Waterville, Maine • London • Munich

For more information, contact
Lucent Books
27500 Drake Rd.
Farmington Hills, MI 48331-3535
Or you can visit our Internet site at http://www.gale.com

LIBRARY OF CONGRESS CATALOGING-IN-PUBLICATION DATA

Thompson, Tamara.
  Emergency response / by Tamara Thompson.
    p. cm. — (Careers for the twenty-first century)
  Includes bibliographical references and index.
  ISBN 1-59018-396-7 (hardcover : alk. paper)
  1. Emergency management—Juvenile literature. 2. Emergency management—
Vocational guidance—Juvenile literature. I. Title. II. Series.
  HV551.2.T48 2004
  363.34'023--dc22
                                                      2004010196

Printed in the United States of America

Contents

FOREWORD   4

INTRODUCTION
  The Circle of Emergency Response   6

CHAPTER 1
  Emergency Dispatchers   9

CHAPTER 2
  Emergency Medical Technicians   24

CHAPTER 3
  Firefighters   38

CHAPTER 4
  Police Officers   54

CHAPTER 5
  Emergency Managers   70

  Notes   89
  Organizations to Contact   94
  For Further Reading   98
  Works Consulted   101
  Index   108
  Picture Credits   112
  About the Author   112

Foreword

Young people in the twenty-first century are faced with a dizzying array of possibilities for careers as they become adults. However, the advances in technology and a world economy in which events in one nation increasingly affect events in other nations have made the job market extremely competitive. Young people entering the job market today must possess a combination of technological knowledge and an understanding of the cultural and socioeconomic factors that affect the working world. Don Tapscott, internationally known author and consultant on the effects of technology in business, government, and society, supports this idea, saying, "Yes, this country needs more technology graduates, as they fuel the digital economy. But . . . we have an equally strong need for those with a broader [humanities] background who can work in tandem with technical specialists, helping create and manage the [workplace] environment." To succeed in this job market young people today must enter it with a certain amount of specialized knowledge, preparation, and practical experience. In addition, they must possess the drive to update their job skills continually to match rapidly occurring technological, economic, and social changes.

Young people entering the twenty-first-century job market must carefully research and plan the education and training they will need to work in their chosen careers. High school graduates can no longer go straight into a job where they can hope to advance to positions of higher pay, better working conditions, and increased responsibility without first entering a training program, trade school, or college. For example, aircraft mechanics must attend schools that offer Federal Aviation Administration–accredited programs. These programs offer a broad-based curriculum that requires students to demonstrate an understanding of the basic principles of flight, aircraft function, and electronics. Students must also master computer technology used for diagnosing problems and show that they can apply what they learn toward routine maintenance and any number of needed repairs. With further education, an aircraft mechanic can gain increasingly specialized licenses that place him or her in the job market for positions of higher pay and greater responsibility.

In addition to technology skills, young people must understand how to communicate and work effectively with colleagues or clients from diverse backgrounds. James Billington, librarian of Congress, ascertains that "we do not have a global village, but rather a globe on which there are a whole lot of new villages . . . each trying to get its own place in the world, and anybody who's going to deal with this world is going to have to relate better to more of it." For example, flight attendants are increasingly being expected to know one or more foreign languages in order for them to better serve the needs of international passengers. Electrical engineers collaborating with a sister company in Russia on a project must be aware of cultural differences that could affect communication between the project members and, ultimately, the success of the project.

The Lucent Books Careers for the Twenty-First Century series discusses how these ideas come into play in such competitive career fields as aeronautics, biotechnology, computer technology, engineering, education, law enforcement, and medicine. Each title in the series discusses from five to seven different careers available in the respective field. The series provides a comprehensive view of what it's like to work in a particular job and what it takes to succeed in it. Each chapter encompasses a career's most recent trends in education and training, job responsibilities, the work environment and conditions, special challenges, earnings, and opportunities for advancement. Primary and secondary source quotes enliven the text. Sidebars expand on issues related to each career, including topics such as gender issues in the workplace, personal stories that demonstrate exceptional on-the-job experiences, and the latest technology and its potential for use in a particular career. Every volume includes an "Organizations to Contact" list as well as annotated bibliographies. Books in this series provide readers with pertinent information for deciding on a career and as a launching point for further research.

The Circle of Emergency Response

Most people, at least once in their lives, will pick up the telephone and dial 911—the national emergency number—to get help. Whether one is calling about a medical crisis, a fire, a car accident, a crime, or another sort of emergency, there is a professional who is specially trained to respond. Because emergencies come in all types and sizes, emergency responders must as well. Emergency response professions are highly specialized. Very different types of training and skills are necessary for jobs in emergency communications, emergency medical services (EMS), firefighting, law enforcement, and emergency management.

Even though the fields are specialized, none of the careers within them are isolated. During an emergency, people in all of these disciplines work closely with one another to complete what one emergency professional calls the "circle of emergency response."[1] There is also a high degree of cross-training among the different professions. Police officers and firefighters, for example, may also be trained as emergency medical technicians (EMTs). Likewise, EMTs might be trained as emergency dispatchers or be members of the fire department's search-and-rescue squad. At the organizational level, a police department might oversee the region's search-and-rescue operations, or the city's hospital may also be home to its 911 communications center. Emergency response professionals from every discipline know that they must work together to get the job done. "Clearly, we all share the same common bond," says police sergeant Ersie Joyner. "We have the same goal in mind: to provide effective service in the situation, whether putting a fire out or responding to a crime in progress. We know what to expect of each other, and we are aware of the resources that each area provides."[2]

It takes a special kind of person to be able to do emergency response work. The work can be extremely demanding, both physically and mentally. Without exception, people who get into this line of work must be able to keep their cool under intense pressure because lives often depend on it. They must be able to make the right decisions quickly and be able to follow through with the correct action. The work can be emotionally stressful as well. People in most of these jobs see horrible things, such as badly injured people, blood, and death.

Being an emergency responder also can be quite dangerous. The terrorist attacks on the World Trade Center and the Pentagon

Emergency responders like these New York firefighters often put their lives on the line. Many emergency responders died in the line of duty during the terrorist attacks of September 11, 2001.

on September 11, 2001, underscore the serious consequences of having a career in this field. More than four hundred firefighters, police officers, and EMS personnel died while doing their jobs that day. But massive calamities aside, the reality is that these professionals face dangerous situations every day, and many die or are injured on the job every year.

Nevertheless, many individuals are drawn to emergency response careers—now more than ever. The main reason is the desire to help people. Whether calming a hysterical caller as a dispatcher, braving a burning building as a firefighter, treating a heart-attack victim as an EMT, tackling a robbery suspect as a police officer, or laying response plans for a large-scale disaster they hope will never come as an emergency manager, all of these professionals do so because of their deep-seated desire to help others.

Chapter 1

Emergency Dispatchers

Nationwide, the 911 emergency reporting number receives some 190 million calls each year—more than five hundred thousand calls a day. The people who answer phone calls to 911 are emergency dispatchers. These people are usually the first emergency officials to find out about a crime, fire, accident, or medical crisis. As the first contact, emergency dispatchers are the pivotal link between emergency responders, such as EMTs, firefighters, and police, and the people who need their help. The emergencies that dispatchers handle can be anything from a fire or explosion to an automobile accident, a drowning, a medical emergency, a lost child, a family dispute, a shooting, or a major event such as an earthquake, tornado, or terrorist attack. "The dispatcher is the first link in the circle of an emergency,"[3] says Victoria William-Jones, a 911 dispatcher with the San Francisco Emergency Communications Department.

Emergency dispatchers go by a number of different job titles. They may be called public safety dispatchers or operators; 911 call takers or dispatchers; emergency communications technicians; emergency medical dispatchers; or police, fire, or ambulance dispatchers. Despite the variety of names, the job is essentially the same.

The Dispatcher's Role in Emergency Response

An emergency dispatcher's primary duty is to take emergency calls from the public and get the right kind of help to the scene as quickly as possible. To communicate with callers, dispatchers use a telephone headset with a microphone. They also have access to many different radio channels to communicate with

Emergency dispatchers around the country handle 911 calls and serve as the central link between emergency responders and those in need of help.

emergency personnel. They sit at a computer terminal, which they use to type in information about the emergency and relay it to others.

Emergency dispatchers work in a variety of settings. The dispatch center may be based in a police or fire station, in a hospital, or in a special city or county communications center ("comm center" for short). Depending on the size of the city or county that the center serves, the number of dispatchers working at a given time may be quite small—just one or two individuals in a small town. In a large city like Los Angeles, however, twenty or more dispatchers often work at the same time.

Regardless of the size of the center in which they work, all centers have what emergency dispatcher and trainer Richard Behr calls a "public safety answering point."[4] That is, the call taker who first answers the phone determines the type of emergency and routes the call to the proper place. In some small comm centers, an emergency dispatcher may be responsible for taking calls as well as dispatching help to the scene. In others, different dispatchers may be responsible for handling different types of emergencies. In such cases, the initial 911 call taker may transfer the call to another emergency dispatcher at an ambulance company or at the police or fire department. In a large center that serves a big city, duties are frequently divided between call takers and dispatchers, who work as a team. "In some agencies, all you do is answer phones. In others, you do everything,"[5] says Behr. Even in agencies where the duties are split, dispatchers typically rotate between call taking and actual dispatching.

However it is organized, emergency dispatchers who answer incoming calls carefully question callers to quickly determine the type of emergency, the exact location of the incident, whether there are injuries, and, if so, how severe they are. If the call is determined not to be an emergency, the dispatcher refers the caller to the appropriate agency to handle the problem on a nonemergency basis.

Because they are the first contact for emergencies of all kinds, emergency dispatchers represent many different kinds of emergency responders. According to Dave Larton, a longtime dispatcher and the associate editor of *911 Magazine,*

> We're paramedics who don't have ambulances. We're police officers that don't wear weapons. We're firefighters who don't drive fire trucks. No matter what the call is, we're really first on the scene. We represent the agency. If our call goes good, then when the officer arrives, when the firefighter arrives, they have a much better chance of handling it as a good call.[6]

Getting the Facts

Besides getting basic information about where the emergency is and what happened, dispatchers need the name of the person who is reporting it and a phone number to call back. If there are victims, the dispatcher must also find out how many people are hurt or ill, their ages, whether they are conscious, whether they are breathing, and whether they have a heartbeat. Dispatchers also frequently ask questions about weapons and drugs to determine whether it is safe to send fire and medical personnel to the scene or whether police should be sent first.

Dispatchers must get this crucial information quickly so that they can send help as fast as possible. That is not always easy because people who call to report emergencies are often upset, scared, or injured, which can make it difficult for them to communicate effectively. Dispatchers, says Behr, "generally deal with people when they are at their worst, or at the worst moment of their lives."[7]

Not being able to see the caller face-to-face also makes communicating more difficult. According to Larton, dispatching is a unique job because, whereas most communication is 85 percent visual, dispatchers rely solely on telephone and therefore cannot see the person they are talking with. Dispatchers, he says, work "literally blind and use [their] voice inflection and questioning techniques to elicit information from the caller, to try to calm them down, and to try to get the right help at the right time to the right place."[8]

Many Rules to Follow

Emergency dispatching is a highly structured job, and dispatchers must follow many rules and regulations. Conversation with callers is heavily scripted, and dispatchers are required to ask for certain information in a certain order. According to William-Jones, "We have written call taking standards we must adhere to at all times. On medical and fire calls, we have a series of protocols we must follow. We are not allowed to pass judgment or offer up an opinion."[9]

In a medical emergency, the call taker/dispatcher frequently stays on the line with the caller and may also give first-aid instructions over the phone until emergency personnel arrive. The dispatcher must closely follow prewritten scripts to ask questions and give instructions. "You cannot deviate from the question unless they don't understand the question and you need to enhance it so they understand,"[10] says Behr. This is done to ensure that the proper questions are always asked and that no instructions are left out, because someone's life could depend on it.

Mobilizing First Responders

Once dispatchers have all of the necessary information about an emergency, they send the appropriate police, fire, or EMS units to the scene, depending on the type of emergency. While a call about a robbery in progress would likely involve dispatching only a law enforcement unit, some emergencies may require the services of many different response agencies. For example, a vehicle accident involving a gasoline tanker truck might require firefighters to put out a fire or free a trapped driver or passenger, EMTs and an ambulance to treat and transport victims, and police officers to determine whether any laws were broken and to direct traffic and keep bystanders in the area safe.

The Civil Service Sector

Although in the past emergency dispatchers typically were part of the fire or police departments, there has been a national trend for public safety agencies to consolidate emergency response activities under a single 911 comm center and to use civilian dispatchers as a way to keep costs down. Those dispatch jobs are considered local or state government positions, also known as civil service. Most emergency dispatch jobs today are part of the civil service system, as are police officer and firefighter jobs.

Besides successfully completing their training, candidates for civil service dispatching jobs are also required to pass a standard civil service exam. This is typically a general knowledge exam that tests such things as reading comprehension, logic, spelling, vocabulary, ability with numbers, and the ability to follow directions. The civil service exam also includes a typing test.

After help has been sent, the dispatcher stays in close contact with the responding units to keep them updated on the situation, to coordinate additional resources, or to arrange to transport victims to a hospital. Dispatchers frequently act as the liaison between hospitals and ambulance crews, giving the hospital updates on ambulance progress as it transports a patient. During a major regional disaster, such as a hurricane, emergency dispatchers work closely with emergency managers to communicate with emergency response agencies, both in their own area and outside of it, to coordinate the needed resources.

Additional Duties

In addition to answering calls and setting response personnel into action, emergency dispatchers must keep detailed logs and records of the calls they receive and the actions they have taken. There is a high level of scrutiny and accountability for their actions. Phone calls to 911 are recorded, and if there is a questionable outcome, the tapes may be reviewed to assess whether the proper decisions were made in a timely manner. It is not uncommon for dispatchers to be called to appear in court to testify about calls they received, actions they took, and what they heard during the call.

Dispatchers who work at dispatch centers that are part of a police or fire department may also be responsible for such things as greeting members of the public who come to the front counter, running warrant or vehicle checks for police units in the field, and processing prisoners into the local jail. According to Captain Richard L. Callen, a dispatch trainer and emergency communications consultant in California, "The smaller the organization, the greater each individual's responsibility has to be. People begin to wear different hats."[11]

"Ready at All Times"

The workload for emergency dispatchers is generally quite demanding. Because 911 phone lines must be staffed with dispatchers 24 hours a day, 365 days a year, emergency dispatchers often must work nights, weekends, and holidays. They typically

During major regional disasters like a hurricane (pictured), communication among emergency managers, dispatchers, and emergency response agencies is crucial.

work eight-hour shifts and may frequently work overtime, depending on how well staffed their agency is and whether there is a major emergency. "When there is a major incident, we are expected to mobilize and come to work for 12-hour shifts," says William-Jones. "The number of personnel needed to handle the flux of calls doubles."[12]

The number of calls a dispatcher handles during a typical shift depends on how much activity there is in the community. In a small town, several days may go by without an emergency call to 911. In a big city, there may be several thousand calls every day. San Francisco, for example, averages about four thousand calls per day. On a busy day, it would not be unusual for San Francisco dispatchers to handle between sixty and eighty calls each. The New York Police Department 911 Center in Brooklyn received more than fifty-five thousand calls on September 11, 2001, following the attack on the World Trade Center—many times its typical call volume.

The busiest shift for emergency dispatchers is usually the swing shift, from 3 P.M. to 11 P.M., when 911 receives the most calls reporting fires, crimes, and auto accidents. The quietest shift is typically the early morning shift, when most people are still asleep and the majority of calls are serious medical emergencies. Nevertheless, emergency dispatchers know that emergencies do not follow the clock. "The nature of this business . . . tells you that anything can happen at any time," says William-Jones.

> We can sometimes anticipate when things will be busy—certain holidays or events create more work for us. We can never predict, however, when a major disaster will strike, when someone will be involved in a major accident, when someone will get ill or a baby will be born. We are just ready at all times.[13]

Roller Coaster of Emotions

Being an emergency dispatcher can be a very rewarding career. Because they play such a key role in getting help to the scene of an emergency, dispatchers have the satisfaction of knowing that they help save lives. "When you do something that directly affects someone's life for the positive, it makes you feel really great,"[14] says Behr.

Nonemergency Calls Clog the System

People who need emergency help depend on 911 dispatchers to be available to answer their calls quickly. Depending on the situation, sometimes even a few seconds' delay can mean the difference between life and death. Frivolous or nonemergency calls to 911 burden the system and may endanger those who have real life-threatening emergencies. Dispatchers receive plenty of these calls, though.

People have been known to call 911 to report trivial problems such as a stubbed toe, a mouse running through the kitchen, a driveway blocked by snow, or a pet parakeet that has flown the coop. Leland Gregory compiled such stories into a book called *What's the Number for 911?* In it, he chronicles some of the oddest calls to come in to emergency dispatch centers. Among the more amusing things emergency dispatchers have heard are "Someone broke into my house and took a bite out of my ham and cheese sandwich," "I'm a hospital patient and I think an orderly wants to see me naked," and "My pig! She's choked and passed out!"

Funny as these kind of incidents might seem, it is no laughing matter for emergency dispatchers, who know that they may be wasting precious time on a frivolous call when someone else who needs real help may be trying to get through. Dispatchers must be able to quickly and tactfully refer nonemergency callers to the proper resources to address their problems.

Though most public safety dispatchers take great pride in their behind-the-scenes role in emergency response, many also acknowledge that it can be extremely stressful as well. Dispatchers endure a great deal of pressure knowing that if they make a mistake on a call, there could be serious—even life-threatening—consequences. "One of the phenomenons of this profession is that you blame yourself when things go wrong. We tend to second-guess ourselves."[15] says Behr, who wrote a book to help dispatchers understand and deal with the traumatic aspects of the job.

Because they must regularly deal with unpleasant and stressful situations, dispatchers frequently experience what Behr calls an "emotional roller coaster" of both highs and lows. For example, a dispatcher may feel great relief and joy when a nearly drowned child starts breathing and crying again after her mother has successfully followed the dispatcher's instructions for rescue breathing. An hour or two later, the same dispatcher may feel devastated by hearing that an accident victim died before help could arrive. According to Behr, all dispatchers "have a moment or type of call that upsets them. It really gets to them emotionally sometimes."[16]

Dispatchers also have a special relationship with the emergency responders they deal with over the radio, and they often feel fiercely protective of them. When bad things happen to the men and women they dispatch to a scene—for example, when a police officer gets shot or a firefighter falls through a roof—it is often quite hard on the dispatchers as well. "We look at our folks out in the field as their protectors," says Behr. "We are like mother hens. We feel responsibility for what goes on out in the field."[17]

Dispatchers occasionally hear things happen over the phone that they cannot do anything about. They may hear screams of

911 dispatchers must often refer nonemergency callers to the proper resources in order to keep their lines clear for actual crises.

pain, cries for help, or worse. When the World Trade Center in New York collapsed after the terrorist attacks of September 11, 2001, many of the victims inside the towers were talking with 911 dispatchers on cell phones. Many dispatchers say the hardest part of the job is the feeling of powerlessness that comes with hearing something happen and not being able to do anything to stop it. Nevertheless, says Behr, "Dispatchers step up to the plate and do the job because that's what they're trained to do."[18]

Skills for Success

Dispatchers need many skills in order to be successful at their jobs. In a written tribute to emergency dispatchers, Loveland, Colorado, police chief Thomas Wagoner sums it up this way:

> Dispatchers are expected to have the compassion of Mother Teresa; the wisdom of Solomon; the interviewing skills of Oprah Winfrey; the gentleness of Florence Nightingale; the patience of Job; the voice of Barbra Streisand or Tom Brokaw; the knowledge of Einstein; the answers of Ann Landers; the people skills of Sheriff Andy Taylor; the humor of David Letterman; the investigative skills of Joe Friday; the looks of Julia Roberts or Tom Cruise; the faith of the Pope; and the energy and endurance of the EverReady Bunny. It is a unique and talented person who can do this job and do it well. Many have tried and failed. It takes a special person with unique skills.[19]

Undoubtedly, the most important quality dispatchers must have is the ability to remain calm under intense pressure. They must be able to calm callers who may be agitated, frightened, or injured. Lives depend on their ability to think clearly and make well-reasoned decisions quickly without panicking. "A good dispatcher is one who is able to stay focused and not become rattled when it gets busy," says William-Jones. She adds, a dispatcher must also be "patient and caring, organized and calm. If the dispatcher displays any unprofessional behavior whatsoever and the citizen notices this, the call can take a spiral turn downward."[20]

Emergency dispatchers must have excellent hearing as well. They need to understand what callers say the first time they give information. Callers may be upset and hard to understand, or there may be background noise or static on the line, so it is criti-

Dispatchers must make quick judgments about the resources needed for a particular emergency. These firefighters were dispatched quickly enough to save this house from ruin.

cal that dispatchers be able to listen carefully and decipher what is being communicated. In an emergency, there is no time to spare to repeat information. Many agencies require prospective dispatchers to take a hearing test; those who do not pass are eliminated from the applicant pool.

Dispatchers must not only be able to hear well but be able to speak well. They must be able to speak English clearly and must have good verbal communication skills so that they can be easily understood. Being able to speak another language, such as Spanish, Chinese, or Vietnamese, is an additional skill that makes a dispatcher particularly valuable, especially in a big city or other area with a large immigrant population.

Since emergency dispatchers have to communicate with callers and often dispatch and monitor the responding units at the same time, it is essential that they be able to "multitask," that

Dispatchers use a system of radio codes as a shorthand form of communication.

is, successfully follow through on several tasks at once. They must be able to enter information into a computer, make quick judgments about what services are needed, dispatch the appropriate resources, and track the movements of responding units—all while talking with the caller. "We need to know where our units are at all times," says William-Jones. "Keeping track of calls and units while dispatching can be challenging. The longer you do the job, the more proficient you become."[21]

Lastly, the quick pace of dispatching work requires proficiency with all of the radio equipment and computers used in the comm center. Public safety dispatchers should be able to type at least thirty to forty words per minute and be comfortable using a computer and radio headset. Good map-reading skills are also useful. Dispatchers must also be able to sit for long periods of time while on duty, and they must be careful to avoid developing repetitive stress injuries to their hands and arms from working on computers under stressful conditions.

Training Requirements Vary

To be considered for a job, emergency dispatchers must be at least eighteen years old and have no felony criminal record. A high school or general equivalency diploma (GED) is the minimum education expected for emergency dispatchers.

Training requirements for emergency dispatchers vary widely. Some agencies have no training requirements whatsoever. They rely on on-the-job training to teach new dispatchers the ropes. Other agencies go the opposite direction and require dispatchers to complete state-recognized training programs or to also be sworn police officers, firefighters, or emergency medical services personnel. Most agencies, though, fall somewhere in the middle. Typical requirements include at least eight weeks of training in emergency call-taking and dispatch procedures, and another four weeks learning to operate the radio and computer equipment. Such training courses are often offered inexpensively at local community colleges.

Some states require dispatchers to be certified through a state-recognized program. When new dispatchers are hired at an agency, the agency typically sends them through the training course for certification. In addition, an in-person interview is always part of any screening process for an agency, and a psychological evaluation, personality test, medical check-up, drug test, and background check may also be required. Once hired, new dispatchers can expect several weeks of closely supervised on-the-job training, wherever they are.

Salaries and Opportunities

Emergency dispatchers—especially those just starting out—make surprisingly little money for the pressure-filled work they do. Starting pay for emergency dispatchers is about $18,000 a year, and the average annual salary falls around $24,000. "The best pay and benefit packages will be with jobs under civil service protection,"[22] says Callen, the emergency dispatch trainer in California. Civil service dispatchers typically make up to $36,000 with three years' experience.

Although there are good opportunities for people entering the field, there is somewhat limited room for advancement within a dispatch center, since the only real upward opportunities are as a dispatch supervisor, trainer, or communications center manager. Every year the *Journal of Emergency Medicine*, an EMS trade publication, puts together an annual survey of salaries in the field of emergency response. Its report for 2000 showed that communications center managers nationwide earned an average of $51,519 a year and communications supervisors earned $40,869.

Saving Lives by the Book

Emergency dispatchers follow scripts when giving lifesaving instructions to callers over the phone. Dispatchers ask specific questions about the victim and, depending on the answers, follow precise guidelines for how to instruct the caller. The guidelines are printed on flip cards so that dispatchers can quickly see the instructions and move between the cards, as the situation requires. The following example of a dialogue that might take place between a caller and an emergency dispatcher when there is an adult choking is drawn from training materials from the New Jersey Office of Emergency Medical Services.

Dispatcher: Is the patient able to talk or cough?

Caller: No!

Dispatcher: Is the patient conscious?

Caller: Yes, but he is grabbing at his throat!

Dispatcher: Stay calm and listen carefully. I'm going to tell you what to do next.

First, stand behind him and wrap your arms around his waist.

Make a fist with one hand and place the thumb side against his stomach, in the middle, slightly above his navel.

Grasp your fist with the other hand.

Then press into his stomach with quick upward thrusts.

Repeat the thrusts until the item is expelled.

If he becomes unconscious, come back to the phone.

Caller: OK, I'll try.

There is a pause for a minute or so and then the caller comes back on the line.

Caller: Oh my God, he passed out! The food popped out, but he passed out and now he isn't breathing!

Dispatcher: You'll need to stay calm if you're going to be able to help him. Listen carefully. I'm going to tell you what to do next. . . .

At this point the dispatcher flips to a different card and follows the guidelines for instructing the caller in adult CPR.

However, aside from positions associated with the 911 reporting system, trained emergency dispatchers may also be employed within police or sheriff departments, fire departments, state or national parks, ambulance companies, and private security firms. Depending on what other skills they possess, some dispatchers may eventually be able to move into emergency management positions. They may also find work as emergency communications consultants for cities, heavy industry, and other large organizations that need emergency communications.

The Future for Emergency Dispatchers

For many years, emergency dispatching was seen as a secretarial position, and it was not until recently that the job began to be viewed as a professional emergency response career. Today, there are more than ninety-seven thousand emergency dispatchers nationwide who are employed in a variety of agencies, including police and fire departments, ambulance companies, and some five thousand centralized 911 dispatch centers. According to the U.S. Department of Labor's Bureau of Labor Statistics, the job outlook for emergency dispatchers appears "excellent in the near future," and there is an expected job growth of "up to twenty percent over the next decade."[23] That is partly due to population growth, because as new areas become populated, they need personnel to handle the increased workload. New positions also become available because the job has a fairly brisk turnover rate. The high level of stress associated with the position often leads to burnout and prompts many dispatchers to leave the job after just a few years. With the expected increase in demand and so many options for employment, emergency dispatchers can expect to enjoy a career that Callen calls "virtually recession-proof"[24]—one that will not be eliminated when the economy is doing poorly.

Chapter 2

Emergency Medical Technicians

Emergency medical technicians (EMTs) are usually the first people with medical training to arrive on the scene of an emergency when someone is ill or injured. The medical crises these emergency response professionals handle vary widely. They may treat victims of heart attacks or strokes, vehicle accidents, near drownings, burns, drug overdoses, gunshot wounds, stabbings, or any other sort of injury or illness. These first responders must be prepared to act quickly to evaluate the situation and save lives. The lifesaving medical procedures EMTs perform vary according to their level of training. There are three levels of certified emergency medical technicians, each more advanced than the last: EMT-Basic (EMT-B), EMT-Intermediate (EMT-I), and EMT-Paramedic.

More than 172,000 EMTs work in the United States today, but the job is not for everyone. According to Mark Lockhart, a paramedic trainer in St. Louis, Missouri,

> It is not an easy job—there is a physical and mental price that may be paid—but the rewards are truly outstanding. There are very few careers where you can do your job and know that you made the difference between pain and comfort, between sickness and health, between life and death.[25]

The EMT's Role in Emergency Response

EMTs provide emergency medical care for sick or injured people at the scene of an emergency and in an ambulance on the way to the hospital. They work together closely, typically in teams of two. EMTs are usually called to an emergency scene by a dispatcher, who has received an emergency call through the 911 reporting system. When he or she arrives at the scene, an EMT's first priority is to quickly identify the nature of the emergency and stabilize the patient's condition until a doctor can take over. According to Patrick Cavanaugh, a paramedic in Pennsylvania, "A Paramedic functions as the eyes and ears of the doctor in the field."[26]

The first thing EMTs always do is take a primary survey by checking the victim's ABCs—airway, breathing, and circulation. They must make sure that the patient has an open airway (the path from the mouth to the lungs), that the person is breathing, and that he or she has a pulse, which means the heart is beating and circulating blood. If the patient is not breathing and does not have a heartbeat, EMTs must immediately work to restore those functions by using cardiopulmonary resuscitation (CPR). To administer CPR, an EMT repeatedly forces fresh oxygen into the victim's lungs and presses down on the chest to force the heart to

An emergency medical technician administers oxygen to a patient as his partners load him into an ambulance. EMTs provide emergency medical care until a doctor can take over.

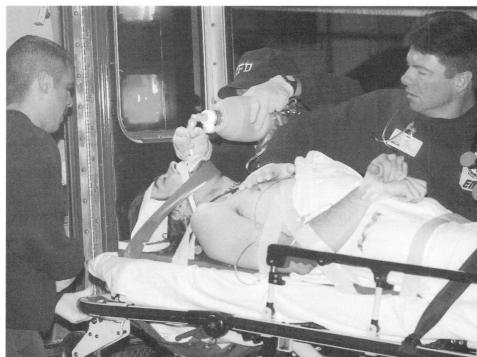

circulate blood to the rest of the body. EMTs have a saying to help them remember how important the primary survey is: "Air goes in and out. Blood goes round and round. Any variation from that is a bad thing."[27]

Once the patient's ABCs have been checked and stabilized, EMTs do a secondary survey, a thorough examination of the patient to determine the extent of the injury or the severity of the illness. If the patient is conscious, EMTs carefully question him or her to determine where the pain is, if the person has any allergies or is taking any medication, and whether he or she is diabetic. If the patient is unable to respond, EMTs question bystanders or family members to get whatever information they can about the patient. "The most common procedures that I perform are the primary and secondary surveys," says Anthony Solorzano, a recently certified paramedic in California. "These surveys provide us with baseline vital [signs] and what treatment protocols to follow."[28] The accuracy of these early assessments is crucial to the patient's chances for recovery.

Lifesaving Skills

The emergency care that EMTs can provide depends on their level of training and what procedures they are certified to do. EMTs of all levels are qualified to check vital signs, such as pulse, blood pressure, and respiration; give CPR; use an automated external defibrillator to shock a stopped heart back into beating; control bleeding and treat wounds; administer oxygen; deliver babies; treat allergic reactions; apply splints to broken bones; and use antishock suits to restore blood flow to shock victims. Those with advanced certifications are allowed to do more complex lifesaving procedures that require greater skill and training. Only the highest level of EMT, a paramedic, can administer drugs, and use heart monitors and other sophisticated medical equipment.

As they treat patients at the scene, EMTs often maintain radio contact with a local hospital or trauma center. Doctors frequently help direct care via the radio, approving advanced procedures as they are needed. According to Alex Kacen, who wrote a book highlighting paramedical careers, "In some cases, conditions are simple enough for you to handle as an EMT on the spot; others are more complicated and can be handled only under the

Lifesaving Levels

There are three levels of EMTs recognized by the National Registry of Emergency Medical Technicians. To maintain their certification level, working EMTs must reregister every two years and meet a continuing education requirement to ensure that they stay up to date on the latest skills and equipment.

EMT-Basic: Most EMTs have only basic certification, called EMT-Basic or sometimes EMT-Ambulance. Training for EMT-Basics typically includes 100–120 hours of classroom work and a 10-hour internship in a hospital emergency room. EMT-Basics can check vital signs (pulse, blood pressure, and breathing); control bleeding and bandage wounds; administer CPR; treat shock; splint fractures; and assist heart attack victims.

EMT-Intermediate: The second level of certification is EMT-Intermediate. Individuals who obtain this level of training can perform more advanced procedures, such as using automated defibrillators to give shocks to a stopped heart, performing endotracheal intubations (from the mouth to the trachea) to assist breathing, and giving intravenous fluids. EMT-I training varies from state to state but typically includes 35–55 hours of additional instruction beyond that of EMT-Basic.

EMT-Paramedic: The highest level of EMT certification is EMT-Paramedic. Training programs for paramedics are extensive, generally lasting between 750 and 2,000 hours. They also usually include an intensely supervised internship in the field. In addition to all of the skills held by the previous levels, paramedics are allowed to administer many different emergency drugs, both by mouth and by giving injections. They can also interpret electrocardiograms (EKGs) to understand heart problems.

step-by-step direction of doctors with whom you may be in radio contact."[29] Likewise, paramedics may use their own judgment about when to administer certain drugs; other drugs require physician approval. "We have a protocol book that tells us what drugs we can give on standing orders depending on the situation, and when we have to call on the radio for direct verbal orders to give drugs,"[30] says Peter Canning, a paramedic in Connecticut.

In the Ambulance

Sometimes, EMTs can provide enough care that the patient does not need to go to the hospital. But if the patient does require hospital care, one EMT drives the ambulance and one rides in back with the patient to provide whatever additional care might be needed. Besides treating victims of emergencies, EMTs are also frequently called on to transport hospital patients from one facility to another and monitor their condition along the way. In the back of an ambulance, says Solorzano, "Our goal is to stabilize the patient. Each patient requires something different."[31] During the transport, EMTs monitor patients very closely. They recheck the vital signs of patients who are in critical condition every five minutes and recheck noncritical patients every fifteen minutes. Some of the other things EMTs may do while en route to the hospital are perform CPR, administer oxygen, give medications or fluids, bandage wounds, or shock heart attack victims to reestablish their heart rhythm.

An EMT monitors a patient in an ambulance en route to the hospital. During the ambulance ride, EMTs ensure that the condition of their patients remains stable.

Once they reach the hospital, EMTs bring the victim into the emergency department and give the hospital staff whatever information they can about the victim's condition. They must also fill out a "run sheet," paperwork documenting the call and what treatment was given.

After the hospital takes over, the EMTs return to their base of operations and prepare the vehicle for the next emergency call by replenishing drug supplies and other equipment. When they are done, they take a careful inventory to make sure they have everything they need for the next call, whenever it comes.

Constantly Changing Environment

EMTs never know what the next call will bring. They work in a constantly changing environment. They may have to work outdoors in extreme weather under very challenging conditions—for example, treating an injured person inside a smashed vehicle in the middle of a freeway on a rainy night. Other calls may bring them into the homes or workplaces of their patients, where they will face an entirely different set of challenges.

Every call is different, and the job literally changes by the minute. Because a medical emergency can strike at any time, ambulance companies and fire departments must be staffed with EMTs twenty-four hours a day. EMTs must be ready to do their jobs at all hours of the day and night. The calls they respond to may be relatively minor, such as a broken bone or a case of the flu, or they may be major events that involve many severely injured people. The volume of cases EMTs handle fluctuates widely, too. "It seems like most serious calls run on the same day—five out of five life-and-death emergencies in a row," says Solorzano. "Then, for the next few shifts, we may have zero lifesaving calls. Overall, I'd say 25 percent of our calls are lifesaving."[32]

Rewards and Risks

Most EMTs thrive on the excitement of the job and derive great satisfaction from being able to help people who are in need. "I think that one of the nice things about this job is that you get so many chances to be nice to people," states paramedic Peter Canning. "There is more to this job than just giving people IVs and medical care. . . . I like being nice to people. Lifting them up lifts me up."[33]

"The Wings of Life"

When EMS crews treat someone whose life is in immediate danger, they may call for an emergency medical helicopter so that the patient can get to the hospital more quickly and receive advanced trauma care on the way. Most big cities now have emergency air transport for trauma victims. The services are usually connected to major regional hospitals and are run by prominent air ambulance companies such as Life Flight or MedStar.

Besides the pilot, the crew on board an emergency medical helicopter typically includes a specially trained flight nurse and an air transport paramedic, who work together to keep patients alive. The craft is specially outfitted with equipment for advanced life support and extreme trauma cases. More than half of the patients transported by emergency medical flights are victims of vehicle accidents.

Flight paramedics undergo much more advanced training than their counterparts on the ground. They must have three years' experience as street EMT-Paramedics as well as certification in advanced life support and advanced cardiac life support. They are also trained in special pediatric life support techniques.

Whereas the calls that most EMTs handle may or may not be severe, a flight paramedic or nurse always has a patient who is in dire need, often critically injured. Flight paramedics must be emotionally prepared to see—and deal with—the worst of the worst. As Robert Nieblas, a flight nurse with Life Flight out of Stanford Hospital in California, told *San Francisco Chronicle Magazine*, in an article titled, "The Wings of Life," "Everything we do, we have to be able to do in a hurry. We're basically working within the confines of the 'golden hour.' In trauma . . . your first hour is the most critical—it's the hour that usually determines whether you live or die."

At the same time that it provides personal fulfillment, the job can be very demanding emotionally. EMTs regularly interact with people who are suffering. They may see terrible injuries, and sometimes patients die despite their best efforts. "I really enjoy being able to help others, but sometimes it gets rough," says EMT-I Ernie Paul.

> I think there is definitely something wrong with a person if what they see as an EMT at an accident scene does not bother them. Sometimes what I see and have to deal with makes me appreciate life more, and sometimes I wonder what is going on with the world. It takes a lot of dedication to perform emergency services for severe incidents, but it's rewarding on the other hand to help someone. They help balance each other.[34]

Besides the emotional strain, the job entails physical risks as well. Because they are regularly exposed to blood and other bodily fluids when treating patients, EMTs must take great care to protect themselves from contracting HIV (the virus that causes AIDS), hepatitis, and other infectious diseases. One of the

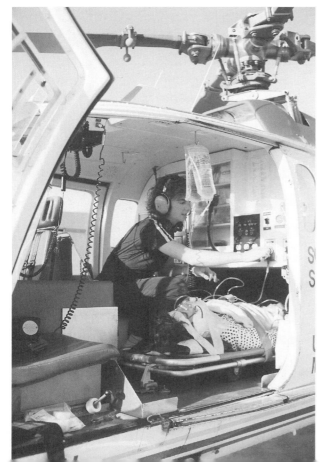

Specially equipped helicopters are used to transport critically injured patients to the hospital.

biggest dangers in this regard is EMTs receiving what is known as a "needle stick," that is, being accidentally pricked by a used needle that has been contaminated by an infected patient. Another common physical risk is back injuries, which can often be career ending and are typically caused by lifting and transferring patients. EMTs may also experience hearing loss from repeated exposure to loud emergency sirens, although many departments now equip their personnel with headsets to block the noise.

Vehicle accidents and crime scenes also pose special hazards for EMTs. They may find themselves in danger from speeding vehicles, crime suspects, or angry bystanders. According to Pat Ivey, a paramedic in Virginia, "Certain calls demand law enforcement—shootings, stabbings, suicides, overdoses. If we're uncertain about the scene being secure, we ask for a deputy."[35] Some EMTs in inner-city areas wear bulletproof vests to protect themselves when responding to medical emergencies that involve shootings.

Skills for Success

Because they work so closely with the public, EMS personnel must have good interpersonal skills. According to Gary Anderson, an EMT trainer from Arizona, "An EMT must be a people person. By that I mean someone who cares for people, their feelings, and their struggle with an emergency situation. An EMT should also have a friendly and team-guided personality to be able to work with other EMTs or fire or police personnel on the scene."[36] People involved in an emergency situation are sometimes very upset, so EMTs often have to calm not only victims but family members and bystanders as well. EMTs must be good listeners and sensitive communicators to do that effectively. Being able to speak Spanish or another language is especially useful.

Having good eyesight and driving skills is important for driving the ambulance, and being physically well conditioned is another crucial factor. EMTs spend a great deal of their time stooping and bending to treat patients, and they must be able to lift heavy loads. Besides being physically fit, EMTs also must be emotionally and mentally prepared to cope with whatever situations they are faced with. They must be able to work under great stress and make quick decisions about how to best handle critical situations. Training is a key part of success in that regard. According to Ivey, "Training displaces fear. So when there is an emergency, we have something to draw on other than being afraid or repulsed. We are more prepared for the unexpected."[37]

Not only do EMTs have to be able to perform advanced life-saving procedures, but they must be able to execute them quickly and flawlessly under intense pressure. "You need to be safe, accurate, and fast," says Solorzano, who adds that that can be harder than it sounds. "Some procedures that are tricky happen so quickly that I don't have time to really think much. I just do it, therefore relying on my training."[38]

Many times, not having time to think can actually be helpful for EMTs. "When I have a lot of time to think things over, doubt creeps in. I start questioning my skills and lose some confidence," says Solorzano. "If I have too much time to think about a call before treating, I get emotionally involved and it becomes difficult to think. After a call like this, if it went OK then I build more confidence in this type of situation."[39]

But the harsh reality is that calls do not always go OK. Sometimes, people die despite the best efforts of EMTs. "If the call didn't go well," says Solorzano, "then I think about what I could have done better and think on this for the next call. . . . We try to be realistic and dismiss the call as 'we did as much as we possibly could to save or help this person.'"[40]

Qualifications and Training

To be admitted into a basic EMT training program, applicants must be at least eighteen years old, have a high school diploma or GED, and have a driver's license. The exact course requirements for the various EMT levels vary slightly state by state. There are many EMT schools around the country, and community colleges typically offer inexpensive programs that include internships in the field.

Paramedic programs require applicants to already have an EMT-Basic certification. Because of the great responsibilities involved in being a paramedic, the education and training process is long and highly supervised. The program can be quite intense, and it typically consists of three parts. The first, called didactic, involves classroom lectures, bookwork, and tests. The

The Elderly and Emergencies

More than a third of all medical emergencies involve someone over the age of sixty. The American Geriatrics Society estimates that about 3.4 million emergency medical calls a year involve older adults. That number will steadily increase over the next three decades as more than 70 million baby boomers (people born between 1946 and 1964) reach retirement age. The problem is, few EMTs are trained to recognize the special problems that aging adults face. The basic EMS course includes only one hour devoted specifically to the elderly; even paramedics get only eight hours of instruction in senior health issues. That is why a new program called GEMS (Geriatric Education for Emergency Medical Services) is being offered to EMS personnel across the country. The idea is to educate emergency medical responders about the special needs of elderly patients. For example, drug interactions, depression, dementia, reduced hearing and sight, and the fear of being put in a nursing home can all impact the health of an aging adult. The new training is important because as baby boomers age, they will become an even bigger part of the patient base for EMTs.

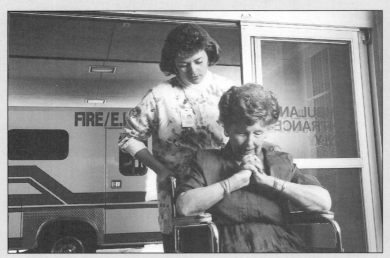

A large number of emergency situations involve the elderly. EMTs must understand their special health needs.

second portion is hospital clinicals, a program of closely supervised hands-on training based in a hospital emergency department. It is during the clinical phase that paramedics learn how to start IVs, inject drugs, and insert breathing tubes down the throats of actual people. The third portion of paramedic training is a field internship. It is the hardest part, says Solorzano, "because you learn to take charge from start to finish. This is an uncontrolled environment, and it can be dirty, smelly, nasty."[41] The internship brings all of a student's book learning and hospital training into practice in real-life emergency situations.

Many people who begin a paramedic training program drop out along the way because it is so challenging. In Solorzano's program, for example, forty people began the training and a year later, only two had acquired their certifications. Ten dropped out for various reasons, and the other twenty-eight were still working on their clinicals or internship.

After all the training in the program is successfully completed, candidates still face another hurdle: passing a state and/or national certification exam. Even after they receive a passing score, paramedical training does not end there. Once a newly certified paramedic gets hired, he or she can count on an on-the-job probationary period of a year or more before working independently. According to Solorzano, who has been on the job just a few months, "Supervision is extremely tight. New paramedics are highly scrutinized. I have to more or less prove myself constantly."[42] And to ensure that their skills are always up to date, EMTs of all levels must pass a rigorous written exam to be recertified, usually every two years.

Salary Depends on Level

How much money EMTs earn depends on their training level, experience, and what kind of employer they work for. Those employed by fire departments receive significantly better pay than those who work for ambulance companies and hospitals because they are usually cross-trained as firefighters. In addition, those who work in large cities typically receive better pay than their counterparts in rural, less populated areas.

According to the *Journal of Emergency Medicine*'s 2000 salary survey, EMT-Basics who worked for ambulance companies were paid an average of $21,614, while those employed by

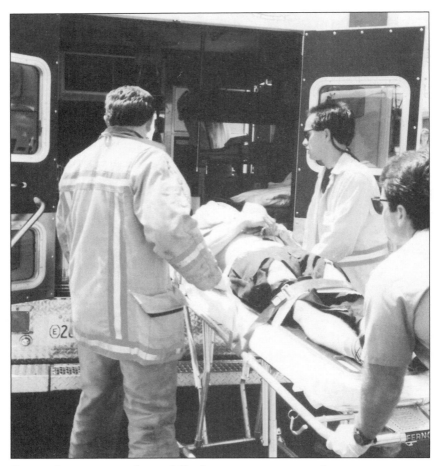

Paramedics must complete a difficult training program and pass a comprehensive exam before being certified to provide emergency medical care.

fire departments made an average of $36,566. The average salary for all EMT-Bs combined was $31,670. For EMT-Intermediates, the average pay was $24,891 with an ambulance company and significantly higher—$35,860—with a fire department. The national average for all EMT-Intermediates combined was $30,283 in 2000. Because of their advanced training, EMT-Paramedics draw the best pay, especially when serving with a fire department. Those at an ambulance company earned an average of $30,020 a year. Paramedics cross-trained as firefighters made more than $12,000 a year extra for an average annual salary of $42,161. The average salary for paramedics working for all employers was $35,689 in 2000.

The Future for EMTs

There were approximately 172,000 EMTs in 2000, according to the U.S. Department of Labor's Bureau of Labor Statistics. Most EMTs were employed by ambulance services and either public or private hospitals. Two-fifths were in private ambulance services; one-third were in municipal, police, or rescue squad departments; and one-fourth were in hospitals. Fire departments are a leading employer of EMTs, especially those with advanced paramedic training. These jobs often require the EMTs to become firefighters as well. There are also many job opportunities for EMTs outside of the traditional emergency response system. Certified EMTs of all levels may find work at clinics, industrial plants and refineries, sports facilities, concert venues, ski areas, and search-and-rescue units, among other places. Event organizers for street fairs and other large public gatherings also frequently hire EMTs. There are also EMT positions within the armed forces and the American Red Cross, a nonprofit disaster relief organization.

EMTs make up one of the fastest-growing career paths in the country. According to the Bureau of Labor Statistics, the field is expected to grow by about 70 percent through 2005. This astronomical growth projection is partially due to the growing population, which makes the demand for services even higher. As demand for services grows, so will the demand for capable individuals to enter this exciting emergency response career.

Chapter 3

Firefighters

Firefighting has come a long way from the "bucket brigades" of the 1600s, in which neighborhood volunteers passed along water-filled buckets to keep their cities from burning down when a fire struck. What began as a volunteer effort to fight fires has turned into a multibillion-dollar industry that today employs about 250,000 full-time paid firefighters and close to 1 million volunteers in the United States alone. Today's firefighters are equipped with sophisticated training, high-tech equipment, and specialized vehicles to help them do their jobs.

The job itself has changed too. Although it is still their main specialty, modern firefighters do much more than fight fires. Broadly put, the job of a firefighter is to protect life and property. Besides fighting fires, they respond to vehicle accidents, industrial mishaps, building collapses, explosions, chemical leaks, natural disasters such as earthquakes and hurricanes, and many other emergency situations. "Firefighters do everything. You cannot separate fires from rescue,"[43] says Dan Green, a fifteen-year veteran firefighter/paramedic in Berkeley, California.

Along with a decreasing emphasis on fighting fires, which has been made possible by the widespread use of smoke alarms and better fire prevention, there is a growing emphasis on providing heavy rescue and medical help as part of the fire department's services. As noted in the *Occupational Outlook Handbook*, published by the U.S. Department of Labor, "Firefighters have assumed a range of responsibilities, including emergency medical services. In fact, most calls to which firefighters respond involve medical emergencies, and about half of all fire departments provide ambulance service for victims."[44] Indeed, actual fires make up less than 20 percent of the workload for modern fire departments. The other 80 percent of the calls firefighters respond to involve medical emergencies or accidents of one sort or another. While the traditional roles of firefighters may be changing, one thing remains the same: Firefighting is still dangerous and difficult work, and it takes a special type of person to fill a firefighter's boots.

The Firefighter's Role in Emergency Response

When they are called to an emergency scene by a 911 dispatcher or other emergency responder, firefighters must be ready to handle whatever they encounter. Because today's firefighters are called on to perform so many different tasks, a clear division of labor and a high degree of specialization are necessary so that they can handle emergency situations effectively. All firefighters have the same basic training to learn how to fight fires, free people

Although extinguishing fires remains the main specialty of firefighters, they, in fact, respond to a wide variety of emergency situations.

trapped in vehicles, conduct search-and-rescue operations, rig rescue ropes, and use firefighting tools, but they do not all perform the same job. Firefighters with similar skills and interests are grouped into "companies" that are associated with certain firefighting tasks, equipment, or vehicles.

Each company plays a unique role in the team effort of firefighting. Depending on what company he or she is part of and whether it is a fire or rescue emergency, the day-to-day job duties of a firefighter vary greatly. According to Green, "Each person is a firefighter but each also has their own particular skill. They have different backgrounds and training to assure they can handle whatever comes up."[45]

Fire Response

Traditionally, all fire departments have an engine company and a ladder (or truck) company. Members of the engine company are primarily responsible for operating sophisticated water-pumping trucks and using fire hoses to direct water onto a blaze. Firefighters on an engine company rarely enter a burning building to search for victims or participate in vehicle rescues. Their skills and duties are particular to the role of wetting down fires and maintaining the vehicles and equipment necessary for that job.

Firefighters on a truck company, by contrast, may go their whole careers without ever being called on to man a fire hose. At a fire, truck company members have one of the most dangerous jobs; they enter burning buildings to search for victims and ventilate the structure. They wear heavy air tanks and specialized clothing to protect themselves from intense heat and smoke. They use tools such as axes, power saws, and crowbars to make holes in the roof and walls so that the fire cannot spread as easily. They may set up fans to pull smoke out of buildings as well. Truck companies are frequently also called ladder companies because their members are also responsible for setting up aerial ladders so that they can get close to or on top of the building to better fight the fire. Finally, truck company members are responsible for overhauling the area after the fire is out to make sure that all of the burning embers are extinguished and that there are no hot spots that might reignite later. They search for

Search and Rescue

Most fire departments have a rescue company or squad whose members are highly trained in specialized rescue techniques. There are many different kinds of rescue situations, and each requires special equipment and expert knowledge of particular tactics. The following are a few of the rescue categories that firefighters can specialize in.

Swift water: People who fall into rushing rivers or storm drains may be pulled out by rescuers using ropes, harnesses, and flotation devices. These rescuers have specialized knowledge about how fast-moving water behaves.

Underwater: Rescuers may use scuba gear and waterproof tools to operate beneath the surface in places such as lakes or reservoirs. This type of rescue might be needed when people are trapped inside a boat or a car that has sunk.

Structure collapse: When an earthquake or other event causes a building to collapse, rescuers who specialize in structural collapse are called to the scene. They are experts in knowing what to move or not move, and in what order. They work to reach people buried in the rubble while keeping the debris pile as stable as possible so nobody else gets hurt.

Winter/Snow: To locate and rescue people who are trapped outdoors in the snow or other dangerous weather, rescuers use all sorts of outdoor survival and mountaineering skills, such as roping, snowshoeing, and ice climbing.

Underground: Rescues in mines, caves, and collapsed trenches require special knowledge of how earth shifts and how air circulates. These rescuers may dig tunnels or do other excavation to reach and free victims trapped underground.

Confined spaces: Rescue in confined spaces is one of the most challenging because of the limited room for equipment and for rescuers to move around. Such a rescue might take place when someone is stuck in a well, drainage pipe, or crawl space of some kind.

Aerial: In an aerial rescue, rescuers may descend by rope from a helicopter to reach someone trapped in a high or otherwise inaccessible place, such as a deep ravine. Typically they then lift victims out by attaching them to a harness or basket.

hidden fire by tearing out parts of walls and insulation and removing debris.

To fight a wildland fire, such as the massive blazes that raged through southern California in fall 2003, firefighters use additional fire-suppression techniques. Besides putting water on the fire, they may dig a "fire line," a trench that serves as a barrier past which the fire cannot spread. They may use chainsaws and axes to clear brush and trees to reduce the material that is available for the fire to consume. They may even light "backfires" to intentionally burn an area to keep a wildfire from spreading past that point. After the fire appears to be extinguished, firefighters again overhaul the scene by turning up brush and cutting back plants to prevent the fire from reigniting.

Everyone Plays a Part

In addition to the traditional truck and engine companies, in the past twenty years, a third company has also become standard: the rescue company. This company is used mainly for nonfire work, such as vehicle accidents, building collapses, and other types of heavy rescue emergencies. In departments that do not have a

Many firefighters are trained in specialized rescue techniques. Here, a group of firefighters rescue hikers from a remote wilderness area.

dedicated rescue company, members of the ladder/truck company have the responsibility for vehicle and heavy rescue activities.

At a vehicle accident, the job of a firefighter is quite different from what it is at a fire, but the same division of labor applies. Everyone has a role to play, and they rely on each other to get the job done. Although treating accident victims is the responsibility of EMTs, who may or may not also be firefighters, accident rescue is the job of the fire department. Both engine and truck or rescue companies typically respond together to rescue emergencies because there is no way of knowing exactly what actions will be needed until they arrive.

Members of the engine company at a vehicle accident are responsible for using hoses and the pumper truck to extinguish a car or brush fire that may have resulted from the accident. The truck or rescue company handles rescuing people trapped in a vehicle. To do this, they use pneumatic (air-powered) cutters and spreaders to cut open the smashed car and use blocks, wedges, or chains to stabilize the vehicle so that it does not move while they are working. Many fire departments also have their own paramedic squad, the members of which are both firefighters and certified paramedics. In this case, the firefighters/paramedics can begin giving medical aid to victims while the rescue is still in progress.

Firefighters clean up the accident scene after the rescue is over. They move debris to the side of the road and use special absorbent materials to mop up oil, gasoline, and other vehicle fluids. They sweep up broken glass and may hose the area down with disinfectant to clean away blood or other unpleasant remnants of the crash.

To further illustrate the various roles firefighters fill, take, for example, an industrial accident in which there is a fire, several injured people, and a man trapped atop a crane with no way to get down. Members of the fire department's engine company would use hoses and operate the pump vehicles to direct water or special chemical foam to smother the fire. Members of the ladder company, meanwhile, would don breathing gear and rush into the building to search for anyone who may be trapped inside. Other ladder truck members would set up aerial ladders so they could climb up to the roof to tear it open to ventilate the fire and slow its spread. At the same time, the fire department's rescue squad would be busy rigging ropes to reach the trapped worker and bring him down, and the hazardous materials squad (or HazMat squad), if the department had one, would be working to identify the various chemicals at the site and evaluate the dangers they pose. Finally, while all of this is going on, the fire department paramedic squad would be treating anyone who was injured. All of these professionals are firefighters. According to retired New York City fire captain William Gates, "Firefighting is a team effort; if one firefighter fails to properly do his or her job, injury or death could occur. We depend on each other for our lives while protecting the life and property of the people of the city."[46]

Life in the Firehouse

The work of a firefighter is not finished once the fire is out or the rescue is over, however. When they are not actively fighting a fire or working on some other emergency, firefighters spend their time at the firehouse cleaning and maintaining equipment, practicing procedures, and undergoing additional training. They may also conduct fire safety inspections in the community and spend time preparing written reports on fire incidents.

While they are on duty, firefighters live together at the firehouse, usually for shifts of twenty-four hours at a time. The station is set up like a home, with a dormitory sleeping area, a shared bathroom, a big kitchen, and a TV room or lounge for socializing. In their free time, the firefighters eat meals together and get as much rest as they can. According to Frank Tijiboy from the Oakland Fire Department, "Unless you're a firefighter, no one can really understand what we do. We have a special relationship. We have to live for 24 hours together. It's not like an eight-hour day where you can put on a fake thing for eight hours and then you go home. Here, this is our home."[47] Indeed, firefighters often spend more time at the station with other firefighters than they do at home with their own families.

Because firefighters live together while on duty and must work closely and practice teamwork, they develop close bonds with each other. According to Gates, "You don't become a firefighter just for the money; it's more than that—much, much more. There is a bond that is shared as in no other profession."[48]

Emergency situations require that firefighters take on well-defined roles. Here, a firefighter on an aerial ladder directs a water cannon onto a raging fire.

Firefighters often describe their coworkers as brothers and firefighters in general as an extended family. Many firefighters say the feeling of brotherhood is the best part of the job. According to firefighter Dennis Smith, "There's a closeness that grows out of being in combat together. Knowing that your life depends on the man working next to you."[49]

That sense of brotherhood also tends to create a special sort of firehouse culture. Firefighters are notorious for their practical joking, especially directed toward "probies"—newly trained and hired firefighters who are on probation for the first six to eighteen months. The jokes and pranks serve as a way to release stress and make new members feel like part of the team.

Risks and Rewards

There is no doubt about it: Firefighting is one of the most dangerous jobs in the country. Many firefighters are hurt or killed on the job each year. That danger was highlighted when 343 firefighters died in the collapse of the World Trade Center towers in 2001. But even in their day-to-day work, firefighters encounter such dangers as collapsing floors and walls, burns, and smoke inhalation. Broken bones and strained backs are common from falls and lifting heavy equipment. They may also be exposed to poisonous gases and chemicals that can have long-term health effects. Because firefighters' jobs are not done until long after the fire is out, they push their bodies to the limit and are often forced to go without sleep for an extended time while working.

Living together creates close bonds among firefighters. They often think of their coworkers as family.

Like those in other emergency response careers, firefighters must often deal with intense emotional stress. As Gates explains, "Conditions at a fire can be brutal, with multiple injuries, [and] people screaming for missing or trapped loved ones."[50] All of that takes a toll on firefighters, and many seek counseling services after especially traumatic incidents to help them deal with their emotions. Firefighters also have a higher than average divorce rate, perhaps because of stress on relationships caused by the high risk involved.

On the positive side, there is a lot of personal prestige in being a firefighter. People view firefighters as heroes, and that can be very rewarding. Firefighters also enjoy being able to help; protecting property and saving lives makes them feel good about their work and themselves. As one firefighter put it, "Firefighters' rewards are found within themselves. Help to the community, loyalty to one's firehouse companions, and the incredible thrill the fire call brings as you turn out [respond to a fire] are the motivators."[51]

Some firefighters even say that the danger of the job can be a blessing because it helps them appreciate life more fully. "I have a different perspective on death now," says firefighter Tina Moore. "Because we see so much death and we hear about death around us, it makes me more conscious of the fact that life is temporary. And for everyone—not just myself being a firefighter, but for everyone—we should live our lives every day, because it might be our last."[52]

Skills for Success

Being a firefighter requires a wide range of mental, physical, and interpersonal skills. Firefighters must be in good physical shape. They must be strong enough to carry a person out of a burning building and have enough stamina to respond to several calls in a single day, often without sleep. Because firefighting is as much mental as physical, firefighters need to learn the chemistry and physics of fire science and be able to apply it in the field. They must work well as part of a team and be able to follow orders without hesitation. Those who aspire to positions as company officers must have good leadership and communications skills. Having a background in mechanics, the construction trades, or heavy machinery is also useful, especially for those interested in heavy rescue.

Firefighters participate in a grueling training session. Firefighters must maintain a high level of physical fitness in order to perform their demanding job.

Education and Training

All firefighters receive their basic training at a fire academy. Training lasts from six to twelve weeks, depending on the department's program. Some employers require firefighters to complete training and be certified before they can be hired; others hire first and then put individuals through the academy. Fire academy

Tools of the Trade

Firefighters use many types of specialized equipment to do their jobs. Two of the most important are the Jaws of Life and SCBAs.

The Jaws of Life: The Jaws of Life are not just one tool. The name refers to several different tools that are used together to cut and pry open vehicles that have been involved in accidents. Cutters are used to cut through the metal, much like bolt cutters do. Spreaders are used to pry it open or tear out a section in its entirety. Rams are used to push sections of metal apart or to brace unstable parts and keep them from shifting. The powerful "jaws" of these tools apply several thousand pounds of pressure and can cut apart a car like it was a soda can. The Jaws of Life revolutionized heavy rescue by dramatically reducing the time it takes to get injured people out of smashed vehicles.

SCBAs: Firefighters trust their lives to SCBAs when they enter a smoke-filled building. SCBA stands for "self-contained breathing apparatus." Firefighters wear these air-filled metal tanks, which look much like scuba diving tanks, on their backs. The tank connects to a face mask that has a breathing regulator. Each tank weighs about twenty-five pounds and contains about thirty minutes of air, although one-hour tanks are also used. Like scuba gear, SCBAs typically include an extra mask to allow firefighters to do "buddy breathing," or share air in an emergency. Many newer SCBA systems transmit information about firefighters and allow someone outside the scene to monitor their air supply and vital signs. One of the drawbacks to wearing an SCBA is that the regulator and mask make it difficult to communicate. However, newer models include voice amplifiers to make talking easier.

teaches recruits the basics of fire suppression, vehicle extrication, search and rescue, and how to stay safe. They learn how to operate specialized firefighting equipment and vehicles and how to follow the chain of command. The academy also includes a rigorous physical conditioning program. Once they are hired as entry-level firefighters, probies can expect several months of close supervision and additional on-the-job training.

Training for firefighters does not stop after the academy and probation period, however; it continues throughout a firefighter's career. Fire departments hold frequent training sessions for their crews to keep their skills fresh and keep them up to date on the latest tools and procedures. In addition to elaborate drills that hone teamwork and technique, trainings known as sign-offs are a regular part of firehouse life. In these trainings, firefighters learn new skills, such as using a new cutting tool, and receive a sign-off that they are certified to do that task.

Most firefighters also undergo additional training so they can be responsible for certain specialized procedures, such as those related to firefighting vehicles, hazardous materials, or search and rescue. The direction their training takes usually depends on their career goals and whether they will work on a ladder, engine, or rescue company. For example, a firefighter who wants to work on a truck company and specialize in search and rescue might sign up for a state-approved program and undergo extensive training in that area. Another firefighter who wants to be an engineer on a pumper truck might take a preparatory course and then take an exam to certify his skills in that role. Firefighters who want to advance upward through the ranks often go back to college to receive a bachelor's degree in fire science. As part of their program, they study such things as physics, building construction, equipment, and firefighting tactics and strategy.

Stiff Competition

Although technically anyone who is at least eighteen years old and has a high school diploma or GED is eligible for consideration as a firefighter, most successful applicants already have a fire science certificate, EMT certification, or an associate or bachelor's degree. The field is fiercely competitive, and there are always many more applicants than open positions. Already having completed training means a better chance of getting hired. According to Jeffrey Cuttitta, a firefighter in Long Island, New York, "It's very challenging to land a job as a full-time career firefighter because there are so many applicants for every open position and there aren't that many open positions available."[53] Many departments, especially those in big cities, also now require all new hires to be certified as an EMT or paramedic because they get so many calls for vehicle accidents and other situations in which medical help is needed.

In many areas, there is so much competition for available jobs that applicants are put on an eligibility list and ranked according to how qualified they are. That eligibility list is then further narrowed based on written, oral, and physical exams. A high percentage of applicants fail one or more of the tests and thus are eliminated from the candidate pool. The one most people fail is the physical test, which re-creates many of the physical tasks firefighters must perform while wearing their heavy protective clothing, known as turnout gear. Women especially have trouble passing this test because it requires a great deal of upper-body strength.

Salaries and Opportunities

Though it is often difficult to begin a career as an entry-level firefighter, there are many opportunities for advancement once a person is hired by a department. The typical pattern of climbing through the ranks from being a level-one firefighter is level-two firefighter, apparatus operator (or engineer), lieutenant or captain, battalion chief, assistant chief, deputy chief, and fire chief. Advancement depends on passing written exams for the position, past job performance, interviews, and seniority.

Salaries vary widely depending on the location, but firefighters are generally paid fairly well wherever they are. In addition to their base salaries, firefighters often earn additional wages for working extra overtime shifts. Nationwide, the average firefighter typically earns between $30,000 and $40,000 annually, with increases coming with seniority and extra training. Firefighters who also have EMT or paramedic training are highly sought after and are typically paid several thousand dollars a year more than regular firefighters in their departments. In 2000 EMT-Basics who worked for fire departments and were cross-trained as firefighters earned an average of $36,566 a year; firefighter-paramedics earned an average of

Women in the Ranks

Even though fire departments actively seek to recruit women, the number of female firefighters is still relatively low. An estimated forty thousand women serve as either paid or volunteer firefighters in the United States—about 3.6 percent of the total, according to Women in the Fire Service, Inc. (WFSI), an organization that tracks statistics on female firefighters. According to the U.S. Department of Labor, just 1.9 percent of career (paid) firefighters employed in 1999 were women. Today, roughly six thousand women currently hold career firefighting positions. California and Florida employ the most female firefighters, and Minneapolis, Minnesota, has the largest female presence on a force: 16 percent.

The first known female firefighter was an African American woman named Molly Williams. She was a slave owned by a member of an engine company in New York City. Although she worked on the early "bucket brigades" that fought fires by passing buckets of water, she never received any pay for her work.

Although fire departments actively recruit women, only a very small percentage of firefighters are female.

$42,160. Apparatus operators, such as those for the engine and ladder trucks, are paid about $5,000 more per year than other firefighters because of their specialized knowledge and greater responsibility. Company officers, such as lieutenants and captains, earn about 25 percent more than rank-and-file firefighters because of their extra responsibilities and management duties. Battalion chiefs, who supervise the fire companies during emergency calls, earn between 10 and 15 percent more than lieutenants or captains do. Average salaries for fire chiefs range from $60,000 to $75,000 annually but can be as high as $100,000 in a big metropolitan area. Firefighters at all levels also typically enjoy a generous benefits package that includes a retirement pension as well as life insurance. Other common benefits include money to clean and purchase new uniforms and tuition assistance for college-level fire studies.

The Future for Firefighters

Ninety percent of the country's 250,000 career (paid) firefighters worked for municipal fire departments in 2000. Some federal and state government agencies, such as the U.S. Forest Service, the Bureau of Land Management, and the state and national park services, also hire full-time firefighters to protect public lands and buildings. Trained firefighters may also find work in the military and in the private sector, especially in the oil, chemical, and aircraft industries. Because fire departments are increasingly competing with other public safety agencies for their share of public funding, few new firefighting jobs are expected to be created through 2010. According to the U.S. Department of Labor's Bureau of Labor Statistics, growth is expected to be slower than average for all professions and will mostly come as volunteer firefighter positions are converted to paid positions.

Even though firefighting is a crowded profession, according to the Bureau, "Fire protection is an essential service, and citizens are likely to exert considerable pressure on local officials to expand or at least preserve the level of fire protection. Even when budget cuts do occur, local fire departments usually cut expenses by postponing equipment purchases or not hiring new firefighters, rather than by laying off staff."[54] That means that once hired, a new firefighter can look forward to a relatively secure career because layoffs are uncommon. Firefighting is a stable career choice even in poor economic times.

Chapter 4

Police Officers

As long as there have been cities, there has been a need for someone to enforce the mutually agreed upon rules of the community. The first law enforcement system in the United States was the volunteer "night watch" that kept law and order in Boston beginning in 1631. The city hired the country's first full-time, paid officers some eighty years later. Today, there are many different types of law enforcement officers at the local, state, and national levels: sheriff's deputies, state troopers, highway patrol officers, federal marshals, FBI agents, and many more.

It is municipal (city) police officers, though, who handle the bulk of day-to-day law enforcement within a community. In 2000 there were more than five hundred thousand police officers in the United States, working for more than twelve thousand municipal agencies. Small rural towns may have just an officer or two, while a big city like New York has several thousand.

Many people are attracted to a career as a police officer because of their desire to serve the community. But being a police officer is not for everyone. According to Officer Christopher Shields from Mississippi,

> Law enforcement isn't a job, it's an unending duty. Once you pin on a badge, once you buckle on your pistol and equipment, once you strap yourself into an Interceptor [a police car], you begin to realize that law enforcement is not a career; it is a calling, one that is heard by only a select, chosen few. The call to serve begins deep inside your heart, way down in your soul, and only you can hear it or answer it.[55]

The Police Officer's Role in Emergency Response

When someone calls 911 to ask for the emergency help of a police officer, it is usually because they have witnessed or been the victim of a crime. An officer's top priority is always responding to such calls for help. In busy cities, 60 to 70 percent of an officer's time is spent answering emergency calls. The rest of an officer's time is spent patrolling the streets or taking nonemergency crime reports.

Requests for emergency police help are ranked by dispatchers or responding officers as A, B, or C priority based on their seriousness. To determine what kind of response is appropriate, officers weigh the gravity of the offense. Calls receive A priority when there is a crime in progress or when there is the risk of someone being hurt. A-priority calls include assaults, rapes, shootings, and other violent confrontations. Other crimes that are still in progress, such as burglaries, are usually also given A-priority status because they can escalate unexpectedly. Whenever

The main responsibilities of municipal police officers are to respond to emergency calls and to patrol the streets of their communities to keep them safe.

When responding to a situation involving an armed suspect, officers use powerful weapons and wear body armor for protection.

police officers use their lights and sirens, it is probably an A-priority call. Responding to A-priority calls is very dangerous for officers because they usually involve confronting dangerous crime suspects who may have weapons. Police often have to chase suspects who try to get away, and officers must frequently rely on martial arts moves, batons, pepper spray, or guns to subdue suspects and arrest them.

B-priority calls are of lesser urgency and are usually property crimes, such as vandalism and car theft. Police try to respond quickly enough to interrupt the crime and catch the suspect, but their main concern is to keep the public safe. Once they can assure public safety, they try to arrest the crime suspect. "If we get there and we catch the suspect, that is great, but we are not going to run the risk of putting someone's life in jeopardy over a property crime,"[56] says Ersie Joyner III, sergeant of police in the patrol division of the Oakland Police Department in California.

Emergency calls about domestic disputes—family arguments— are the most common calls that police officers respond to. They are also frequently the most volatile, even though they are usually considered B priority. "Throughout a police officer's career, this is probably the number one most dangerous type of call to go on because they are so unpredictable,"[57] says Joyner. The danger lies in the fact that most of the time the victim is just as agitated as the suspect. Officers rely on their skills as mediators to de-escalate these disputes whenever possible.

As the lowest priority call for police help, C-priority calls involve crimes that have already happened and which simply require a police officer to make a report. C-priority calls are usually property crimes in which the suspect is long gone and there is no continuing threat to the public. These crimes would include the theft of a bicycle or car stereo or graffiti painted on a building. Officers respond to C-priority calls as they are able to fit them in around other, more immediate, calls for help.

First Responders

Besides being the primary responders for crime-related emergencies, police officers also play a major role at many other types of emergency scenes. Police are summoned for everything from car accidents to drug overdoses to fires, and because they are already out patrolling the community, they are often first on the scene. "A lot of times, an officer is put in the position of not only being a law enforcement officer but also being the first to render medical assistance or locate victims. It is a dual role; we wear many hats,"[58] says Joyner.

Throughout their shifts, police officers are in constant contact with dispatchers as they receive calls for help, update dispatchers about their location and the situation, ask for information about suspects, and call for backup help from fellow officers. In many situations, police officers work closely with other emergency responders such as EMS personnel and firefighters. At a scene where other responders such as firefighters or paramedics have the lead role, police officers secure the situation and make

it safe for them to do their jobs. That might mean directing traffic at the scene of a vehicle accident or keeping bystanders from
interfering with rescue efforts. "Many times," notes Joyner, "medical or fire cannot respond until we give them the all clear."[59]
Police officers assisting at a fire or accident also investigate the
scene and interview witnesses to determine whether any crime
occurred.

Different Every Day

The primary duty of police officers is to uphold the law, but how
they do that duty changes constantly. As one police officer puts
it, "Few other jobs may start the day with a high-speed chase or
end it taking drugs away from people who don't want to give
them up."[60] Police officers never know what they will encounter
during their patrol shift.

A police officer's day typically starts with a briefing by the
sergeant from the prior shift to update incoming officers on what
is going on in their area. Officers are then given their patrol
assignments, and after they check their equipment and vehicles,
they hit the streets. Officers who work in municipal police
departments have general law enforcement duties, meaning that
during any given shift they may pursue and arrest crime suspects;
serve arrest warrants (an order from a judge to arrest someone);
secure a crime scene; interview victims, witnesses, and suspects;
pull people over for traffic violations; issue citations for various
offenses they witness; mediate family arguments; fingerprint suspects; or provide traffic and crowd control at public events.

When they are not actively responding to calls for help,
police officers patrol the streets looking for problems. They keep
an eye out for suspicious circumstances, things that might be a
hazard to public safety, or individuals who are breaking the law.
Officers usually patrol with a partner, but in a rural area they are
more likely to patrol alone. The territory a police department
serves is usually broken down into different "beats," specific areas
that officers are assigned to patrol. Patrol officers usually travel
around the community in a police car, which is equipped with the
latest communications technology and computers to help them
identify suspects and communicate with other officers and dispatchers. Some officers, though, patrol on a motorcycle, bicycle,
or horseback instead.

Besides their day-to-day patrol work, police officers often have to testify in court about the crimes they witness, the suspects they arrest, and the procedures they follow. Officers must keep meticulous records of what has happened during their shift and must write detailed reports whenever they handle an incident or arrest someone. Some departments are also responsible for providing staffing for the local jail.

In addition to being patrol officers, police can follow many different paths of specialization. Some officers specialize in things such as police-dog handling, bomb disposal, or special weapons and tactics (SWAT). Others work with units that specialize in fighting certain kinds of crime, such as identity theft, computer crime, or gang activity.

A Life of Duty

Because police protection must be provided to a community twenty-four hours a day, officers often work weekends, holidays, and nights. Police officers are expected to report for work whenever their services are needed, even if they were not scheduled for duty. In addition, officers are generally expected to enforce the law when necessary, whether they are on or off duty. This makes a law enforcement career more of a way of life than a job.

Officers often patrol the streets on motorcycles, allowing them to pursue suspects on terrain not suitable for automobiles.

Skills for Success

Because the main emphasis of their job is interacting with people in all sorts of situations, police officers should like meeting people and working with the public. Being able to communicate effectively is very important, and speaking a foreign language is always an asset. According to Joyner, "Law enforcement involves constant communication, whether it's with fellow officers, dispatchers, victims, witnesses, or suspects."[61]

Police officers must be able to follow orders and they must have good moral integrity; they should be honest and reliable and have sound judgment. They are trusted with a very awesome power over others, and they must be able to use it fairly and wisely. Keen observation skills and a memory for details are important so that officers can accurately recount what they have seen and done, in both their written reports and court testimony. Good writing skills are essential as well. Ongoing physical fitness, stamina, and agility are also necessary because officers may have to climb fences, chase crime suspects, and perform many other physical tasks during the course of their work.

A Dangerous Job

Most jobs in emergency response have an element of physical danger, but the danger that a police officer faces is quite different from what other professionals encounter. Not only can police officers get hurt on the job in all of the usual ways, but people may purposely try to kill them. "I've been shot at. I've shot at people. I've had my partner shot. I've had just about everything happen to me in my career,"[62] said Joyner. He added that when he works a beat in a high-crime area it is not uncommon for him to draw his gun two or three times during a shift. According to an officer from another state, "There are people out there that just do not like police officers. It is just that simple. There are people who will never like police officers no matter what you say or do. And there are people who just *hate* cops—period!"[63] The sobering reality is that police officers are often in the unenviable position of being a target.

That said, how dangerous police work is greatly depends on the location. Being an officer in a large urban center with a high crime rate like Detroit or Los Angeles is far more risky than

SWAT Officers

Special weapons and tactics (SWAT) officers are highly specialized members of the police department. SWAT officers are specially trained to handle extreme situations that a regular police officer may not be equipped to deal with. SWAT officers respond to crises such as hostage situations, suicidal crime suspects, high-risk arrests, barricaded suspects, and terrorist attacks. Theirs is among the most dangerous jobs in law enforcement.

SWAT officers train extensively in firearms and marksmanship, building entry, search techniques, and arrest procedures. They also are experts at such activities as lowering themselves from helicopters, rappelling from rooftops, and climbing up buildings and other structures. These officers undergo constant training to hone their skills. Some of the things they regularly practice are hostage rescue, active shooter scenarios, and moving around an area without being seen.

The equipment SWAT officers use includes high-powered rifles and other specialized weapons, night-vision devices, lighting systems, shields and battering rams, noise and flash diversion devices, and climbing gear. SWAT officers wear special protective equipment, including helmets, face shields, and full body armor that covers the torso, legs, and arms. Sometimes a SWAT team travels in its own armored personnel carrier, a bulletproof vehicle.

Rappeling down a building or cliff is just one of many specialized skills required of SWAT officers.

patrolling a much quieter suburban or rural area. When high- and low-crime areas are averaged, national estimates show that the typical municipal police officer draws his or her gun only twice during his or her entire law enforcement career. The odds of actually having fired it are even slimmer.

Crime statistics notwithstanding, directly confronting criminals is not the only danger police officers face. Vehicle accidents are another major hazard, and there are also the unpredictable risks inherent in being a first responder. The deadliest day in law enforcement history was September 11, 2001, when seventy-two officers were killed in the collapse of the World Trade Center towers as they helped victims try to evacuate.

Stress Comes with the Territory

Like other careers in emergency response, police work can be very stressful. Many police officers see people suffer and die because of criminal behavior and accidents. After shooting incidents or other tragedies, officers are required to go to stress debriefing so

Police officers line up for role call as they begin an active and stressful day. Many of them thrive on the excitement of their work.

they can talk about their emotions. Nevertheless, even with the availability of counseling, the stress of being under the constant threat of harm can take its toll on an officer's private life. Police officers have one of the highest divorce rates of any occupation, by some estimates as high as 60 percent.

The flip side of stress, however, is excitement. Police officers often have personalities that thrive on the excitement of police work, and they derive great pleasure from the stimulation that comes with the job. Joyner is far from alone in saying that "Even to this day, I get the same adrenalin rush that I did when I was a younger officer. It keeps me safe. It heightens my awareness and makes me cognizant of what is going on around me."[64]

Because the job of an officer frequently involves acting against the will of another person, such as when making an arrest, it can feel like a thankless position. According to Officer Don Farley from Virginia, "Being an officer is much like being an umpire in a game. No matter what decision you make, someone is going to be upset. An officer must be able to interpret the law so that the people involved have an understanding about the action you have taken."[65]

Many officers say that, despite the risks, they enjoy their work because it gives them an opportunity to serve their community and stop some of the bad things from happening to people. It is a career that is its own reward. Joyner put it this way: "If you join the police department because you are looking to get thanked, you are choosing the wrong career. That is not the reason you're in the game. Gratification comes when you do something well and you know that you helped someone."[66]

Many Requirements

Being a police officer is a position of great trust within a community, so officers must meet strict criteria in order to serve. Candidates must be U.S. citizens, be at least twenty-one years of age (usually), have no felony convictions, have a high school diploma or GED, and be able to pass a civil service exam (a general knowledge exam that tests such things as logic, spelling, math, and the ability to follow directions). Besides the minimum qualifications, police candidates are also held to very rigorous physical and personal standards. Police departments intensely screen candidates to make sure that they are physically capable of performing the job and that they have the right type of personal character to be a police officer. The screening process usually includes a written exam, psychological testing, a thorough background investigation, physical agility and strength testing, and oral interviews. Most applicants are also subjected to lie detector tests and drug screening. The screening process is so rigorous in many places that out of every hundred applicants, only one will be hired and ultimately trained to be a police officer.

Stiff Competition

There is a great deal of competition for entry-level police jobs, meaning standards are high and employers are very selective. Having some education past high school betters chances of getting hired. Many police departments pay an annual bonus to officers who have a degree, and others now actually require it as a condition of hiring. Some departments will even pay for their officers to work toward degrees in criminal justice, administration of justice, police science, or public administration. Many junior colleges, colleges, and universities offer two- or four-year degree programs in these areas.

Another thing that can give candidates an edge in hiring is military experience. Police departments are organized much like the military, with similar discipline and a hierarchy of ranks and command responsibilities. According to Dana Johnson, a police officer in Virginia, "The one thing that helped me become a police officer was serving four years in the U.S. Navy . . . . For other people I strongly urge them to go into the military to be taught the discipline that a police academy cannot always teach."[67]

For individuals who are not yet twenty-one, one way to prepare for a career as a police officer is through a police cadet program. Many departments have such programs for high school graduates who are under the minimum police hiring age. Cadets are hired to do police department clerical work, and they receive training to be officers, usually over the course of two years. When they are old enough and have met all of the requirements, they can be appointed to the force.

Police Academy

Once a candidate is hired by a police department, he or she must complete a police academy program, which usually takes twelve to fourteen weeks. It is at the academy that recruits learn how to do all of the duties required of a police officer. They receive extensive training in such things as proper police behavior, patrol tactics, traffic control, using firearms, self-defense, and emergency response. The training also includes instruction in constitutional law and civil rights, laws, and accident investigation. Officers in police academies nationwide are given training in basic first aid and CPR as well. Many departments also sponsor officers for additional EMT-Basic certification.

The police academy is an intense experience that has been likened to military boot camp. Recruits are put through a rigorous physical training program in addition to learning police techniques and doing classroom work. "It is like having a full-time job forty hours a week and then coming home and having another full-time job on top of that. What they push is training, training, training,"[68] says Joyner. Police academy is so difficult, he added, that of the thirty-two people in his training class, only eighteen graduated and ultimately got their badges. The training does not end with a police academy diploma, however.

Long hours of classroom instruction combined with extensive field training are necessary to acquire the skills needed to become a police officer.

K-9 Cops Take Bite out of Crime

One special type of police officer is a K-9 handler. These officers work with police dogs as their partners. Both the dog and the human officer are specially trained to work as a team when responding to crimes and other emergencies. The dogs are full-fledged police officers, and their handlers are handpicked to be their partners. The two undergo extensive training together. Being a K-9 handler is a highly sought-after specialty within police work.

Police dogs, which are known as K-9 units, typically ride along with police officers as they patrol by car. They are used to track or search for suspects who may be running or hiding, and then subdue them by barking or biting until their human partner can take over. The dogs are also frequently trained to detect drugs or explosives. Their main job, though, is to protect their handler, whether given a command to help or not. K-9 officer Jock Coleman from the Oak Ridge Police Department in Oak Ridge, Tennessee, works with a German shepherd named Nix. A local newspaper called the *OakRidger* did an article about Coleman and his canine partner titled "A Day in the Life: Police Officer Nix's Daily Routine Not a Dog's Life." In it, Coleman told the paper that his canine partner is "really in tune to what's going on. . . . He knows I need him and he has to be there—right now."

Some K-9s are specially trained to work with handlers who are SWAT officers. Tactical K-9s frequently wear special bulletproof dog vests, and they may even do such things as rappelling (being lowered on ropes with the aid of a harness).

Being a K-9 officer is a special job that does not end when the work shift is done for the day. Police dogs live in their handler's home, and the two share a very close bond, both on the job and off. "This is a dog I have entrusted my life to," says Coleman. "He's not my pet. He's my partner." After the dogs retire, they usually continue to live with their human partners.

Besides playing a big role in fighting crime, K-9 units also do a lot of educational and training demonstrations in the community. In many areas, the dogs and their handlers are a key part of good police department public relations.

When a new officer comes out of the academy, he or she is paired with a field-training officer for three or four months. Field training serves as an extension of the academy. Rookie officers are constantly tested in real-life situations, and their training officer evaluates their actions. Training officers typically encourage the rookies to do the majority of the work so that they can apply their training and get practical exposure. It takes a while before they are trusted as full-fledged partners. "Before someone actually gives you the seal of approval, you have to show that you are a well-rounded officer," reports Joyner. "Things must be proven." According to Joyner, all of the training serves one purpose: "When you're placed in life-or-death situations, you have to make split-second decisions and you're not afforded the opportunity to analyze the situation. Through training, repetition, and practice, you can do what you need to do."[69]

Even after competing the academy, police officers continually work to develop their skills, and training is a regular part of their job. Officers receive ongoing training in such areas as sensitivity and communications skills, self-defense, firearms, use-of-force policies, crowd-control tactics, legal developments, and new equipment.

Good Salaries and Opportunities

Police officers are generally well compensated for their work. According to the U.S. Department of Labor's Bureau of Labor Statistics, police officers nationwide had median annual earnings of $39,790 in 2000, with beat officers typically earning between $31,410 and $43,450. Opportunities for advancement within a police department are quite good. Promotions to corporal, sergeant, lieutenant, captain, and chief usually are based on seniority, a written exam, and job performance. Along with such promotions in rank come additional prestige, responsibilities, and compensation.

According to the International City-County Management Association's annual Police and Fire Personnel, Salaries, and Expenditures Survey, the average pay for full-time higher-rank positions in 2000 was as follows: police chief, $62,640–$78,580; deputy chief, $53,740–$67,370; captain, $51,680–$64,230; lieutenant, $47,750–$57,740; sergeant, $42,570– $50,670; corporal, $35,370–$43,830.

An armed FBI agent patrols a federal office building. A position with the FBI is one of several job opportunities in law enforcement available at the federal level.

Police officers at all levels often work additional shifts to earn extra money. Overtime pay can be quite significant, and the take-home pay of officers is usually much higher because of it. Police officers usually also receive a good benefits package that includes paid vacation, sick leave, medical and life insurance, and a uniform allowance. A police pension, a type of retirement plan, is one of the special perks of being a police officer. A police pension frequently allows officers to retire at half salary or more after only twenty or twenty-five years of service. Because of this, many officers look forward to the opportunity to pursue a second career while still in their forties.

Where the Jobs Are

According to the U.S. Department of Labor's Bureau of Labor Statistics, 834,000 police officers and detectives were employed in 2000. About 80 percent were employed by local governments, such as cities and counties. Metropolitan police departments employ more officers than any other type of law enforcement agency.

There tend to be more qualified candidates than job openings in federal and state law enforcement agencies but not enough people to fill openings in many local and special police departments. In other words, municipal police departments are the best bet for finding a job in law enforcement. Hiring opportunities are best in departments that offer relatively low salaries or urban communities where the crime rate is relatively high. Competition is keen for higher paying jobs in more affluent areas.

Individuals with experience as police officers may also find positions as officers in public school districts, universities, and transportation systems or as sheriff's deputies, correctional officers, private detectives, and security guards. The state and federal governments also have a wide range of law enforcement positions. Opportunities at the state level include state troopers or highway patrol officers. Those at the federal level include FBI and Drug Enforcement Administrative (DEA) agents, Secret Service agents, U.S. marshals, and border patrol agents.

The Future for Police Officers

Through 2010, employment for police officers is expected to increase faster than the average for all other occupations. The main source of new police jobs is expected to be officers who retire, transfer to other jobs, or stop working. Concerns about terrorism, drugs, and a trend toward a more security-conscious society are also expected to contribute to the demand for police services. Growth is likely to continue as long as crime remains a concern, but employment for police officers depends on the level of government funding. Public safety is a taxpayer priority, however, and layoffs are uncommon because typically there is a great deal of political pressure to see that police services not suffer cutbacks. "We are a necessary entity because people don't want to live in fear of crime," says Joyner. "Suspects need to know there's someone who will stop them. Police officers have to be both truth seekers and stuntmen or stuntwomen—a superhero. It is the perfect career."[70]

Chapter 5

Emergency Managers

Emergency managers do exactly what their name implies: They manage emergencies. Although usually overlooked as part of the circle of emergency response, an emergency manager is a key player in the response to large-scale emergencies such as earthquakes, hurricanes, floods, major fires, and terrorist attacks. These emergency professionals take charge of a big disaster at many levels—before, during, and after it happens. "The job of an emergency manager is important because no one else sees the 'big picture'—how all the agencies fit together in a coordinated response to a disaster,"[71] says Jim Aldrich, emergency services coordinator for the city and county of San Francisco.

In the field of emergency management, professionals who have similar job duties may be employed at the local, state, or federal government levels and may go by many different titles. They may be called emergency preparedness coordinators, disaster preparedness coordinators, emergency or disaster planners, emergency services coordinators, disaster response coordinators, or hazard or crisis planners or managers. However, the term preferred by most professionals in this quickly growing field is emergency manager.

The Emergency Manager's Role in Emergency Response

When a large-scale emergency happens, the main job of an emergency manager is to synchronize the emergency response efforts of dispatch, fire, police, and EMS instead of having them work alone and without coordination. "Firefighters put out fires and rescue people, police officers and sheriff's deputies enforce the

How Response Agencies Work Together

CHAIN OF COMMAND
Generally speaking, decisions during a disaster or other big emergency are made at the local level. The city or county emergency management office, through its Emergency Operations Center, is in charge of coordinating the efforts of first responders and disaster relief agencies for even the biggest catastrophes. When it needs more help, emergency managers at the local level ask the state's office of emergency management to send workers, money, or equipment. The state, in turn, may seek help from the Federal Emergency Management Agency (FEMA), an arm of the federal government that is part of the U.S. Department of Homeland Security.

FEDERAL
Department of Homeland Security

Federal Emergency Management Agency (FEMA)

STATE
Emergency Management Agencies

Emergency Operations Centers (EOCs) ←→ **CITY OR COUNTY** Emergency Management Agencies

FIRST RESPONDERS
• Emergency Medical Services (EMS)
• Police Department
• Fire Department
• Search & Rescue Units

DISASTER RELIEF AGENCIES
• Red Cross
• Salvation Army
• Community Volunteers

law and maintain order, and emergency medical responders provide care on the scene of a disaster and transport victims to hospitals," says Aldrich. "Once disaster strikes, emergency managers work behind the scenes to ensure that the responders have the resources they need and that all the agencies working together on the incident are coordinating their efforts."[72] That can be a lot more complicated than it sounds.

There are four phases to the job of emergency management: response, recovery, mitigation, and preparedness. Although the duties of a local (city or county) emergency manager change significantly during each phase, one thing that remains constant is the manager's role as a link between emergency responders, volunteer disaster relief organizations (such as the Red Cross), and state and federal emergency management agencies.

Response

The most visible role of an emergency manager is during the response phase of a disaster. Response activities begin during an emergency or soon after it happens. During this phase, the top priority is to handle the immediate problems resulting from the situation—to rescue people, treat the injured, extinguish fires, and so forth. According to Aldrich, "Emergency managers run the emergency operations center (EOC), where decisions about things like evacuation and sheltering, curfews, school closings, and use of resources are made."[73]

A crucial part of what emergency managers do is establishing and coordinating "mutual aid," help from emergency response agencies that are outside of their area. Emergency managers use the EOC as a base to direct an overall response effort involving police, fire, EMS, and specialized rescue units from outside the area as well as those from the city's own emergency crews. Emergency managers must monitor emergency resources from many different agencies. They keep close track of what responders are working on what tasks and what equipment and manpower is still available. They work very closely with police, fire, and EMS officials to recommend the use of personnel, equipment, and supplies, and they share their overall emergency response plan with everyone involved.

To help emergency managers do their jobs, the emergency operations center is typically equipped with state-of-the-art com-

During large-scale emergencies, the primary responsibility of emergency managers is to coordinate the efforts of dispatch, fire, police, and EMS.

munications gear, computers, and audiovisual equipment. The center often includes such things as computerized wall maps and traffic monitoring systems. The EOC serves as a command hub for emergency and city officials of all kinds. "All public safety and emergency response agencies send representatives there to coordinate the overall response,"[74] says Aldrich.

Besides coordinating emergency responders, another primary focus of the response phase is providing help for people who have lost their homes or have other pressing issues. People who survive a major catastrophe may need many things. The most important needs are medical help, food, shelter, and trauma counseling. Survivors are also likely to need things such as clothing, shoes, blankets, and bathroom facilities. Information is also very important to disaster victims; they need information about what happened, what to do next, how to get reunited with loved ones, and what services are available to them.

Emergency managers work with mutual aid agencies and volunteer disaster relief organizations such as the American Red Cross or Salvation Army to meet all of these needs. They help coordinate emergency medical care, shelter, and food for victims. They may also help establish sanitation facilities, direct the distribution of emergency supplies, or provide emergency warnings and instructions to the public. They also manage staging areas for emergency responders—places where they can get tools, fuel, food, medical care, or simply take a shower and rest.

One of the unique aspects of the job involves tapping into different resources—that is, getting help from departments that are not typically part of the circle of emergency response. For example, emergency managers might work with a city's parks and recreation department to arrange shelter facilities for victims or work with the human resources department to screen and register volunteers.

During a crisis, emergency managers also provide information for the news media to share with the public, and they frequently brief government and community leaders on the progress of the response. Finally, every disaster response that takes place serves as an opportunity to review existing plans and see what can be improved for the next time. As Aldrich explains, "After the event is over, the emergency manager will reconvene the group to conduct an after-action review to see what lessons can be learned for future emergencies."[75]

In addition to putting their efforts into high gear during a major catastrophe, emergency managers often respond to smaller emergency events, such as missing person searches and multi-alarm fires. Besides keeping them in practice for a larger emergency, they allow emergency managers to keep up on what is happening in the field.

Recovery

After the immediate needs of disaster victims have been met, recovery activities begin. During the recovery phase, emergency managers work to improve the overall situation so that life can get back to normal for most people. Some of the things that might happen during the recovery phase include helping victims find more permanent housing arrangements, tearing down and removing damaged buildings, rebuilding roads, and restoring services such as electricity and water.

The American Red Cross

The American Red Cross is a nonprofit disaster relief organization that responds to more than sixty-seven thousand emergencies in the United States every year. The Red Cross is always one of the first agencies to help a community after a natural or man-made disaster. The types of disasters that the Red Cross helps with range from large scale disasters such as hurricanes to house or apartment fires in which people have lost their homes and belongings. Because there are thirteen hundred Red Cross chapters located all over the country, the Red Cross can respond to a disaster within two hours, no matter where the trouble is.

Red Cross disaster relief focuses on meeting the needs that people have immediately after a big emergency, such as shelter, food, medical help, and counseling services. The main goal of the Red Cross is to help individuals and families get back on their feet after an emergency. The Red Cross also feeds emergency workers, helps concerned family members outside the disaster area communicate with their loved ones, provides blood and emergency medical supplies, and helps disaster victims access other available resources.

American Red Cross chapters across the country provide shelter, food, medical attention, and counseling to disaster victims.

A supply truck brings relief to flood victims. Emergency managers ensure that adequate resources are available to respond to all types of catastrophes.

Emergency managers continue to operate from the command center during this time. They work closely with government officials and various emergency response agencies to make decisions and coordinate resources. "The emergency manager is a very important adviser to the mayor of a city or to a county executive when tough decisions need to be made about recovering from a disaster,"[76] says Aldrich. City or county emergency managers remain in close contact with other emergency managers at the state and federal levels to arrange for help in the form of money, workers, or equipment to aid the community's recovery.

Mitigation

There is an old saying, "An ounce of prevention is worth a pound of cure." It means that taking a little time to prepare for something that could go wrong is better than spending a lot of time fixing it after it does. Emergency management professionals live by that motto probably more than anyone else. When they are

Anticipating Disaster

Emergency managers spend much of their time planning for things that they hope will never happen. The range of events they have to be prepared to respond to is extremely wide. It includes both natural and man-made disasters, which can be either accidental or deliberate. Each type of catastrophe requires a different type of plan and a different type of large-scale response. Some of the events an emergency manager would be involved in handling include the following:

- Hurricanes and other extreme storms
- Earthquakes
- Tornadoes
- Volcanic eruptions
- Major industrial accidents
- Toxic spills or the release of poisonous gases into the air
- Airplane crashes
- Building collapses
- Power blackouts
- Interrupted water service
- Civil unrest, such as a riot
- Train accidents
- Heat waves and droughts
- Bridge or freeway collapses
- Coastal damage caused by ocean waves
- Terrorist events, such as bombings
- Landslides and mudslides
- Floods and flash floods
- Large search-and-rescue operations
- Interrupted supplies to the community, such as food and fuel
- Nuclear power plant accidents
- Major fires and explosions
- Gas leaks
- Oil spills
- Infectious disease epidemics

not actively working on the response or recovery phases of a disaster, emergency managers try to find ways to prevent a disaster from happening in the first place. If they cannot do that, they search for ways to reduce the effect a disaster might ultimately have on a community. This is called mitigation. During this phase, managers study disasters to understand how and why they happen and to see if there is anything they can do to prevent them or lessen the damage the next time.

One of the main ways they do this is to focus on what some people in the emergency management field call "disaster by design." The idea is that the way buildings are designed and cities are arranged has a lot to do with how vulnerable they are to damage during disasters. By working with engineers and city planners, emergency managers can identify disaster risks and find ways to minimize them. That might mean testing buildings and freeways to see if they are strong enough to survive a big earthquake or making sure that houses are not built in low-lying areas that are likely to flood. It could even mean creating a warning system to tell people who live near a refinery to stay indoors when dangerous chemicals are released into the air. In all of these examples, lessening the danger or reducing the damage is the main goal.

Other aspects of mitigation include teaching ordinary citizens how to help their families, friends, and neighbors during an emergency. Emergency managers often hold training classes for community members and help them form groups that can assist during a crisis, such as Community Emergency Response Teams. They may also work with businesses and nonprofit agencies to establish clear roles for the next time there is a disaster.

Preparedness

Finally, when emergency managers are not involved in response, recovery, or mitigation activities, they spend their time preparing for things that might happen and making plans for exactly how they will respond. During this quieter phase of the job, emergency managers research and create detailed emergency plans for just about every kind of threat that a community could face—everything from volcanic eruptions and hurricanes to train derailments and nuclear power plant accidents.

This phase of the job revolves around updating and revising existing written response plans and developing new plans. To do this, emergency managers take part in extensive meetings with staff from different agencies who are knowledgeable about the many topics a plan must address. Disaster preparedness is most successful when many agencies work together and share plans and ideas. The emergency manager gathers response plans from all the agencies and departments and uses them to produce one overall response plan for the entire area. A great deal of knowledge and experience goes into developing such a plan. According to Aldrich, "Planners must know a lot about how the different public safety agencies respond, how they work together and communicate with each other, what resources they need, and how citizens are affected by emergencies. Not much is kept secret, since we all feel responsible for each other's communities."[77]

Building and maintaining good relationships with all of the different emergency response agencies is one of the most important aspects of the emergency management job. Emergency managers at the local level maintain close relationships with the American Red Cross, the Salvation Army, and other disaster relief organizations, known collectively as VOAD (Voluntary Organizations Active in Disaster). Emergency managers at the state level handle most contact with state agencies, such as the department of transportation, as well as federal agencies like the Federal Emergency Management Agency (FEMA).

City or county emergency managers interact constantly with dispatchers and first responders to refine their plans and practice disaster skills. During the preparedness phase, emergency managers talk almost daily with 911 dispatch supervisors to understand the kinds of calls generated by events that occur in the community. Because they must be ready to put their plans into action at a moment's notice, emergency managers make it a point to know what is going on in each of the emergency response agencies. They know roughly how many dispatchers, paramedics, firefighters, and police officers are working; how many vehicles are available; and who has what type of special equipment.

Training Is Crucial

Another major part of preparedness is training. Once response plans are made to address the possibility of a particular catastrophe happening, emergency managers develop training programs for both emergency personnel and community members.

Emergency managers play a big role in training not only the emergency management staff that will help run the emergency command center but frontline emergency responders as well. Emergency managers work closely with fire and police commanders to train them in emergency management principles and the incident command system, a set of standard procedures that makes it easier for professionals from different agencies to work together during mutual-aid events.

Once everyone is trained on a specific disaster response plan and knows their role, emergency managers conduct simulated dis-

Emergency managers oversee simulated disaster exercises with emergency responders from different agencies. Here, a staff member playing an uncooperative woman is dragged from a building during a drill.

aster exercises with emergency responders from all of the different disciplines. The drills can be quite elaborate, with piles of debris set up to simulate a collapsed building and actors used to play the parts of trapped or injured victims. Emergency managers often add surprise elements to the drills, such as announcing that a second disaster has taken place or that a key command participant has been killed. This is done to test the flexibility of the system and see how responders adapt to unexpected changes. Such exercises give everyone involved practice in large-scale, multiple-agency response so they know what to do during a real emergency.

Public education is also an important component of any preparedness effort. Emergency managers frequently speak to schools and businesses about preparing for and recovering from disasters. And emergency management departments at all levels of government offer training programs, such as FEMA's community emergency response teams, to teach citizens how to prepare for disasters and be able to help in their aftermath.

New Focus

Responding to natural disasters such as earthquakes and hurricanes has traditionally been the primary focus of emergency management. In recent years, however, man-made disasters—whether accidental or intentional—have dramatically increased the importance of this field and reshaped its duties. In particular, the September 11 attacks on the World Trade Center increased the emphasis emergency managers put on man-made disasters. According to Michael Fagel, an emergency manager who helped create an emergency plan for cleaning up the World Trade Center site, "Emergency management has come of age in this series of horrific events."[78] The biggest change is the new focus on homeland security and developing plans to respond to terrorist attacks.

Many in the field of emergency management worry, however, that the new emphasis takes away from planning for more likely events, such as earthquakes, tornadoes, and hurricanes. A natural disaster is still far more likely to hit a community than a man-made one. Officials estimate that most people will be directly affected by a natural disaster at least once in their lives.

In the past, the emphasis was mostly on responding to a disaster after it happened, but today's emergency management professionals understand the importance of trying to anticipate a disaster and lessen the harm it causes. "The effects of any kind of disaster or major emergency on communities seems to be greater and greater as time goes on," says Aldrich. "Cities are recognizing how important mitigation is to prevent and minimize the effects of disasters."[79] This shift of focus toward mitigation, coupled with the emphasis on man-made disasters, has redefined the job of an emergency manager and will continue to shape the field well into the future.

Risks and Rewards

The bigger and more widespread a disaster is, the more emotionally devastating it can be, especially when many people are suffering or have lost their lives. Stress, fatigue, and burnout are the greatest risks associated with the job of an emergency manager. During an emergency event, emergency managers may work for many hours nonstop and may have to do without sleep for an extended period of time. In addition, what is expected of an emergency manager during a crisis may be simply overwhelming. "There is too much going on [in an emergency] for one person to manage," says Aldrich. "The answer is to learn to delegate [assign tasks to people] effectively."[80]

Because emergency managers are not as visible to the public as other emergency response professionals, they often receive little praise or public recognition for their efforts. Their reward is a personal one that comes from gaining the respect of their peers and the satisfaction of knowing how to help in a time of turmoil. "The job is still very much behind the scenes and 'invisible' to the public," says Aldrich. "There is not much prestige, but we all realize how important our jobs are."[81]

Skills for Success

To succeed as an emergency manager, good communication skills are essential. The job centers on being the link between different groups of people, so the ability to form good relationships, share ideas, and work as part of a team is critical. Emergency managers must be good listeners, have patience, and be able to make sound decisions under a great deal of pressure. They should be detail oriented and be able to keep track of many things happening at the same time.

Although the focus of emergency management has shifted to man-made disasters since September 11, 2001, natural disasters remain a priority. Here, disaster relief workers prepare supplies for hurricane victims.

Because a good portion of the work involves writing detailed plans and other documents, good writing ability and computer proficiency are also important. Emergency managers must have good public speaking skills as well, since they often speak before government officials, the press, and the public. Geography, mapping, or amateur radio skills are helpful too, as are teaching and project management abilities.

Growing Education Opportunities

Traditionally, people have entered the field of emergency management because they have been exposed to similar responsibilities in police or fire departments or the military. Some come from the American Red Cross or other nonprofit agencies, and many have experience as disaster relief volunteers. Up until recently, there was little in the way of formal instruction specific to emergency management. But all that is changing because of the new emphasis placed on both man-made disasters and mitigation.

That is good news for anyone interested in emergency management. Ten years ago, there were only five colleges in the United States that offered emergency management certificates or degree programs. Over the past few years, such programs have mushroomed. Today, forty-seven states have at least one college-level emergency management program; fourteen universities offer bachelor's degrees in the subject; and several offer master's and doctorates. According to Bernard J. Dougherty from Western Carolina University, which offers an emergency management degree program,

> Disasters have occurred since biblical times and, in one form or another, have impacted or affected almost every region on earth. Despite this fact, a formal academic approach toward preventing, mitigating, managing and recovering from disasters—both natural and man-made—only recently began. And, in the aftermath of the events of Sept. 11, 2001, offering students an opportunity to pursue careers in this field has taken on new importance.[82]

Much of the push for formal education programs in emergency management is backed by FEMA, which is working with educators to define professional standards for the field. "The emergency manager of today is very different from the civil defense director of many years ago. A major change took place," says Wayne Blanchard, manager of FEMA's Higher Education Project. On the Web site for the project, Blanchard describes the new type of emergency manager as needing a well-rounded education in emergency management, unlike his predecessors. Blanchard advises students "to enroll in a solid degree program and to focus on the development of a broad range of skills—many of which boil down to interpersonal communication and recognition that networking and coordination are more important than command and control. I would stress the need to pick up the tools and skills that would be needed to not only succeed in the field but to become leaders in it."[83]

In addition to its involvement in furthering emergency management through higher education, FEMA offers extensive Internet courses in the field. Its online Emergency Management Institute offers in-depth instruction that can be completed at one's own pace from home. FEMA also offers formal instruction at its training institute in Emmitsburg, Maryland. In addition, most states have some sort of emergency management training institute that is affiliated with or approved by the state office of emergency management. The International Association of Emergency Managers, a worldwide professional organization for emergency managers, also sponsors a certified emergency manager program.

Volunteering Is Valuable

Besides formal education, volunteer work is an indispensable component of preparing for a career in emergency management. Volunteer opportunities that relate to emergency management can be

Get CERT-ified

One way for those interested in the field of emergency management to get some experience is to take part in FEMA's Community Emergency Response Team (CERT) program. The CERT program trains people to prepare for emergencies and to respond to disasters in their communities. CERT members learn how to assist emergency responders, provide aid to victims, and organize volunteers to help during a disaster. The training covers disaster preparedness, disaster fire suppression, basic disaster medical operations, light search and rescue, disaster psychology, and how to work as part of a team. It also includes a disaster simulation that lets participants practice what they learned. The free program is twenty hours long, spread out over seven weeks.

The CERT program was started by the Los Angeles City Fire Department in 1985, and FEMA made the training available nationally in 1993. Today, there are more than 340 CERT programs in forty-five states, and so far more than two hundred thousand people have completed the training. The program is usually offered through a local police or fire department or an office of emergency management. The FEMA Web site (www.fema.gov) has an area dedicated to CERT and it lists the programs by state. Although those under eighteen are usually welcome to participate, some areas may require a parent to go through the training too.

found with the American Red Cross, the Salvation Army, youth programs such as Fire Explorers or Police Cadets, scouting, or the Civil Air Patrol, among others. The city, county, or state office of emergency management might also offer volunteer opportunities. Becoming a lifeguard or taking first aid and CPR training is also a good way to start.

Where the Jobs Are

Jobs for emergency managers can be found at every level of government and throughout the private sector as well. Federal and state laws requiring communities to develop emergency plans and conduct preparedness activities have spurred the demand for those educated in emergency management.

At the federal level, the main agency dealing with disaster planning and emergency preparedness is FEMA, which is now part of the U.S. Department of Homeland Security (DHS). There are extensive opportunities within FEMA and the DHS for individuals with disaster preparedness, planning, and response skills. In addition, most other federal agencies have emergency managers who are in charge of coordinating disaster preparedness and response for the particular agency.

At the state level, each state is required by law to have an office or department of emergency management. State emergency management offices may go by several different names, such as department of emergency services. They usually have at least one emergency manager and several emergency planners and other disaster specialists. Most cities and counties throughout the country also have an office of emergency management. In a rural area, the department may consist of just one or two individuals, while in a big city or urban region it may be an entire staff of emergency managers, planners, and coordinators.

In the private sector, airports, schools, hospitals, sporting arenas, transportation agencies, and heavy industries all employ emergency managers. Those who have experience in this field may also work independently as emergency management or risk reduction consultants.

Salaries

The pay range for emergency managers varies widely depending on the duties they assume and the level of government at which

Emergency managers work at every level of government. Here, a FEMA manager (right) and his colleagues deal with 2002's tropical storm Isidore.

they work. At the local level, the size of the city or county, as well as its affluence, influences the pay scale. Those working as emergency managers in a small town in a rural area might earn only $20,000 or so per year, whereas those in a heavily populated city or county could expect to make more than $50,000. The pay is a little higher at the state level, but again it depends on the size and relative wealth of the state. Pay for those who work in a state office of emergency management ranges from around $30,000 to $70,000. Working as an emergency manager at the federal level—for example, at FEMA—brings the highest salaries. Federal emergency managers make between $45,000 and $90,000, depending on the responsibilities their positions entail. Some emergency managers work in the private sector as consultants. They are able to set their own fees based on their experience and the scope of their work.

The Future for Emergency Managers

The job of an emergency manager, as it is today, is a relatively new profession that is growing quickly. According to Aldrich, "The field of emergency management continues to develop rapidly as disasters and major emergencies become more frequent and responses to such emergencies become more complex."[84] That growth is expected to continue as long as keeping the public safe from large-scale disasters remains a government spending priority. Opportunities to enter and advance in emergency management are expected to increase along with increases in government funding for homeland security.

Recent laws requiring communities to have disaster preparedness and response plans also mean that more jobs are being created in this field and that jobs currently held by volunteers or part-timers may soon become full-time professional positions. As it stands right now, there are not enough qualified people to fill all of the new positions that are being created, which is good news for those interested in pursuing this type of career. According to FEMA's Blanchard, "We will need a new generation of more professional, diverse and better-educated emergency managers, in both the public and private sectors, and more 'disaster sensitive' professionals in other fields to better face the challenges posed."[85]

Notes

Introduction: The Circle of Emergency Response

1. Victoria William-Jones, interview with author, San Francisco, CA, June 13, 2003.
2. Ersie Joyner III, interview with author, Oakland, CA, November 25, 2003.

Chapter 1: Emergency Dispatchers

3. William-Jones, interview.
4. Richard Behr, interview with author, Riverside, CA, June 11, 2003.
5. Behr, interview.
6. Quoted in Gary Allen, "Chief Gates Hosts On-Line Talk on Dispatching," *Dispatch Monthly*, 1999. www.dispatch monthly.com/stories/other/gates_show.html.
7. Behr, interview.
8. Quoted in Allen, "Chief Gates Hosts On-Line Talk on Dispatching."
9. William-Jones, interview.
10. Behr, interview.
11. Richard L. Callen, *Become a 911 Dispatcher: Your Personal Career Guide*. Orange, CA: Career, 1997, p. 1.15.
12. William-Jones, interview.
13. William-Jones, interview.
14. Behr, interview.
15. Behr, interview.
16. Behr, interview.
17. Behr, interview.
18. Behr, interview.
19. Thomas Wagoner, "A Tribute to Dispatchers," April 25, 2000. www.nd.edu/~dnemeth/ODE.html.
20. William-Jones, interview.

21. William-Jones, interview.
22. Callen, *Become a 911 Dispatcher*, p. 2.3.
23. U.S. Department of Labor, Bureau of Labor Statistics, "Dispatchers," *Occupational Outlook Handbook*, 2002–2003. www.bls.gov/oco/print/ocos138.htm.
24. Callen, *Become a 911 Dispatcher*, p. ix.

Chapter 2: Emergency Medical Technicians

25. Quoted in Alex Kacen, *Opportunities in Paramedical Careers*. Chicago: VGM Career Horizons, 2000, p. ix.
26. Quoted in Dennis V. Damp, *Health Care Job Explosion*. Moon Township, PA: Bookhaven Press, 1998, p. 101.
27. Quoted in RescueHouse.com, "Rules of EMS," www.rescue house.com/content/emsjokes/000007.php.
28. Anthony Solorzano, interview with author, Fair Oaks, CA, September 7, 2003.
29. Kacen, *Opportunities in Paramedical Careers*, p. x.
30. Peter Canning, *Paramedic*. New York: Fawcett Columbine, 1997, p. 36.
31. Solorzano, interview.
32. Solorzano, interview.
33. Canning, *Paramedic*, p. 282.
34. Quoted in Cheryl Hancock, *EMT Career Starter*. New York: Learning Express, 1998, p. 20.
35. Pat Ivey, *EMT: Rescue!* New York: Ivy Books, 1993, p. 55.
36. Quoted in Hancock, *EMT Career Starter*, p. 14.
37. Ivey, *EMT*, p. 47.
38. Solorzano, interview.
39. Solorzano, interview.
40. Solorzano, interview.
41. Solorzano, interview.
42. Solorzano, interview.

Chapter 3: Firefighters

43. Dan Green, interview with author, Oakland, CA, February 1, 2004.

44. U.S. Department of Labor, Bureau of Labor Statistics, "Firefighting Occupations," *Occupational Outlook Handbook.*

45. Green, interview.

46. Quoted in Mary Masi, *Firefighter Career Starter.* New York: Learning Express, 1998, p.iii.

47. Quoted in PBS.org, "Life of a Firefighter," www.pbs.org/testofcourage/life.html.

48. Quoted in Masi, *Firefighter Career Starter*, p. v.

49. Quoted in Mary Price Lee and Richard S. Lee, *Careers in Firefighting.* New York: Rosen, 1993, p. 52.

50. Quoted in Masi, *Firefighter Career Starter*, p. v.

51. Quoted in Lee and Lee, *Careers in Firefighting*, p. 5.

52. Quoted in PBS.org, "Life of a Firefighter."

53. Quoted in Masi, *Firefighter Career Starter*, p. 165.

54. U.S. Department of Labor, "Firefighting Occupations."

Chapter 4: Police Officers

55. Christopher T. Shields, "Why I Became a Police Officer," 2000. www.goingfaster.com/tourofduty/why.html.

56. Joyner, interview.

57. Joyner, interview.

58. Joyner, interview.

59. Joyner, interview.

60. Mary Hesalroad, *Law Enforcement Career Starter*, 2nd ed. New York: Learning Express, 2001, p. 7.

61. Joyner, interview.

62. Joyner, interview.

63. Quoted in Life on the Beat.com, "Police Academy—Frequently Asked Questions," http://lifeonthebeat.com/police_academy.htm.

64. Joyner, interview.

65. Quoted in Hesalroad, *Law Enforcement Career Starter*, p. 9.

66. Joyner, interview.

67. Quoted in Imagiverse, "An Interview with Dana Johnson," January 25, 2002. www.imagiverse.org/interviews/dana johnson/dana_johnson_25_01_02.htm.

68. Joyner, interview.

69. Joyner, interview.

70. Joyner, interview.

Chapter 5: Emergency Managers

71. Jim Aldrich, interview with author, San Francisco, CA, December 3, 2003.

72. Aldrich, interview.

73. Aldrich, interview.

74. Aldrich, interview.

75. Aldrich, interview.

76. Aldrich, interview.

77. Aldrich, interview.

78. Quoted in Karen Thompson, "The Importance of Investing in a Sound Emergency Management Program," International Association of Emergency Managers, 2002. www.iaem.com/EM_Promo_Article_2002.pdf.

79. Aldrich, interview.

80. Aldrich, interview.

81. Aldrich, interview.

82. Quoted in *Asheville Citizen-Times*, "New Emergency Management Degree Program Good Step Toward Protecting Vulnerable Public," January 15, 2003. http://cgi.citizen-times.com/cgi-bin/print/26852.

83. Quoted in Karen Thompson, "FEMA Higher Education Project Manager Discusses the New Generation of Emergency Managers," *IAEM Bulletin*, May 2000. www.dola.state.co.us/oem/Publications/prep2001-C.pdf.

84. Aldrich, interview.

85. Quoted in Thompson, "FEMA Higher Education Project Manager Discusses the New Generation of Emergency Managers."

Organizations to Contact

American Ambulance Association
8201 Greensboro Dr., Suite 300, McLean, VA 22102
(800) 523-4447
www.the-aaa.org
e-mail: secretary@the-aaa.org

The American Ambulance Association represents ambulance services across the country. It works to improve medical transportation and emergency medical services and also offers job postings for available EMS positions.

American Red Cross
2025 E St. NW, Washington, DC 20006
(202) 303-4498
www.redcross.org

The American Red Cross is a humanitarian organization that helps victims of disasters. It also teaches people to prevent, prepare for, and respond to emergencies. The Red Cross offers training and volunteer opportunities in communities nationwide.

Association of Public-Safety Communications Officials, International (APCOI)
2040 South Ridgewood, South Daytona, FL 32119-8437
(904) 322-2500
www.apcointl.org
e-mail: apco@apco911.org

APCOI is a union that represents emergency dispatchers and other public safety communications professionals. Its Web site includes articles and background material as well as job postings.

Disaster News Network
7855 Rappahannock Ave., Suite 200, Jessup, MD 20794
(888) 203-9119
www.disasterresponse.net
e-mail: info@villagelife.org

Disaster News Network is a news service that specializes in stories about disaster response and suggests ways the public can help survivors. Its Web site includes listings of volunteer opportunities in disaster relief.

Federal Emergency Management Agency (FEMA)
500 C St. SW, Washington, DC 20472
(202) 566-1600
www.fema.gov

FEMA is the federal government agency in charge of preventing, preparing for, and responding to disasters. The organization offers extensive online training programs in emergency management and has a wealth of information about the field.

International Association of Fire Fighters (IAFF)
1750 New York Ave. NW, Washington, DC 20006
(202) 737-8484
www.iaff.org

This is the primary union to which paid firefighters belong. It advocates for firefighters and offers opportunities for training.

National Academies of Emergency Dispatch (NAED)
139 East South Temple, Suite 530, Salt Lake City, UT 84111
(800) 960-6236
www.naemd.org

NAED is a nonprofit organization that promotes emergency dispatch services worldwide. NAED supports research and regulation for first responders, and it works to strengthen the emergency dispatch community through education, certification, and accreditation.

National Association for Search and Rescue (NASAR)
4500 Southgate Pl., Suite 100, Chantilly, VA 20151-1714
(703) 222-6277
www.nasar.org
e-mail: info@nasar.org

NASAR is an association for people involved in search and rescue, either professionally or as volunteers. The group offers extensive resources and training programs and is dedicated to advancing professional, literary, and scientific knowledge in fields related to search and rescue.

National Association of Emergency Medical Technicians (NAEMT)
408 Monroe St., Clinton, MS 39056
(800) 34-NAEMT
www.naemt.org
e-mail: info@naemt.org

NAEMT is a professional organization for EMTs. It provides educational programs and works to establish national standards for care.

National Association of Police Organizations (NAPO)
750 First St. NE, Suite 920, Washington, DC 20002
(202) 842-4420
www.napo.org
e-mail: info@napo.org

NAPO is a coalition of police unions and associations from across the United States. It works to advance the interests of America's law enforcement officers through legislative and legal advocacy, political action, and education.

National Center for Women and Policing (NCWP)
433 S. Beverly Dr., Beverly Hills, CA 90212
(310) 556-2526
www.womenandpolicing.org
e-mail: womencops@feminist.org

The NCWP works to increase the number of women at all ranks of law enforcement. Its goal in doing so is to improve police response to violence against women, reduce police brutality and excessive force, and strengthen community policing reforms.

National Flight Paramedics Association (NFPA)
383 F St., Salt Lake City, UT 84103

(800) 381-6372

www.flightparamedic.org

NFPA is a professional organization for paramedics, specifically those who treat and transport patients in helicopters or airplanes. The group's mission is to increase the knowledge base and professionalism of their specialization.

National Registry of Emergency Medical Technicians (NREMT)

6610 Busch Blvd., Columbus, OH 43229

(614) 888-4484

www.nremt.org

e-mail: webmaster@nremt.org

This organization is responsible for registering certified EMTs nationwide. Its Web site is a great resource for learning about EMT testing requirements.

National Volunteer Fire Counsel (NVFC)

1050 17th St. NW, Suite 480, Washington, DC 20036

(888) 275-6832

www.nvfc.org

e-mail: nvfcoffice@nvfc.org

NVFC is a nonprofit membership association for volunteer fire, EMS, and rescue services. The NVFC provides information about legislation, standards, and regulatory issues for volunteers.

For Further Reading

Ronny J. Coleman, *Opportunities in Fire Protection Services*. Chicago: VGM Career Horizons, 1997. Details the different fire-related career opportunities and their training and hiring requirements.

Dennis V. Damp, *Health Care Job Explosion*. Moon Township, PA: Bookhaven Press, 1998. Details various career paths in the health-care field, including those in emergency medicine.

Paul C. Ditzel, *Fire Engines, Firefighters*. New York: Crown, 1976. A comprehensive history of firefighting, from the colonial days through the 1970s. This book puts special emphasis on historical equipment and vehicles.

Leland Gregory, *What's the Number for 911? America's Wackiest 911*. Kansas City, MO: Andrews McMeel, 2000. A collection of funny, nonemergency calls that came in to the nation's 911 emergency reporting centers.

Cheryl Hancock, *EMT Career Starter*. New York: Learning Express, 1998. Handbook explaining EMT careers and how to pursue training and job placement.

David Hayes, ed., *Exploring Health Care Careers*. Chicago: Ferguson, 1998. Overview of many different careers in the health field, including interviews with people actually doing the jobs.

Mary Hesalroad, *Law Enforcement Career Starter*. 2nd ed. New York: Learning Express, 2001. Explains the various career paths in law enforcement and offers a detailed explanation of how to prepare for and successfully begin a career in the field.

Pat Ivey, *EMT: Rescue!* New York: Ivy Books, 1993. A firsthand account of the daily dramas of working on a paramedic rescue crew.

Alex Kacen, *Opportunities in Paramedical Careers*. Chicago: VGM Career Horizons, 2000. A career guidebook detailing the different paramedical career opportunities and their requirements.

Mary Price Lee and Richard S. Lee, *Careers in Firefighting*. New York: Rosen, 1993. Provides an overview of the history, duties, equipment, and various positions within fire protection services. Includes a chapter devoted to women in firefighting.

Eve Marko, *Clara Barton and the American Red Cross*. New York: Baronet Books, 1996. A biography of the founder of the American Red Cross and a summary of the organization's history and its present-day role in disaster relief.

Mary Masi, *Firefighter Career Starter*. New York: Learning Express, 1998. Explains the various career paths in firefighting and offers a detailed explanation of how to prepare for and successfully begin a career in the field.

Randy Narramore, *How to Become an Emergency Dispatcher*. 2nd ed. Public Safety, 1996. A step-by-step guide for preparing for a career as an emergency dispatcher. Includes sample oral review board interview questions.

Linda Peterson, *Careers Without College: Emergencies*. Princeton, NJ: Peterson's, 1993. A brief look at the various careers in emergency services that are available to those without a college education.

Barry D. Smith, *Rescuers in Action*. St. Louis, MO: Mosby, 1996. A book full of dramatic photos of the many different types of search-and-rescue operations. Exciting photography but very little text.

Works Consulted

Books

Richard Behr, *Under the Headset: Surviving Dispatcher Stress.* Temecula, CA: Staggs, 2000. A book written for emergency dispatchers to help them understand and cope with job-related stress.

Richard L. Callen, *Become a 911 Dispatcher: Your Personal Career Guide.* Orange, CA: Career, 1997. Career guidebook for aspiring emergency dispatchers; explains duties and education requirements and provides resources.

Peter Canning, *Paramedic.* New York: Fawcett Columbine, 1997. A firsthand account of what it is like to be a new paramedic during the first year on the job.

Carol Chetkovich, *Real Heat: Gender and Race in the Urban Fire Service.* New Brunswick, NJ: Rutgers University Press, 1997. A well-researched survey of the politics, policies, and personal struggles surrounding gender and race within fire departments nationwide.

Harlan Gibbs and Alan Duncan Ross, *The Medicine of ER.* New York: BasicBooks, 1996. A look at whether the medical procedures and outcomes depicted on the TV emergency drama *ER* are realistic or not.

Janice Hudson, *Trauma Junkie: Memoirs of an Emergency Flight Nurse.* Buffalo, NY: Firefly Books, 2001. A firsthand account of what it is like to be an emergency flight nurse.

Dennis S. Mileti, *Disasters by Design: A Reassessment of Natural Hazards in the United States.* Washington, DC: National Academies Press, 1999. This book provides an overview of natural hazards and disasters as well as response and recovery efforts. It focuses on minimizing hazards to create disaster-resilient communities and also examines disaster losses over the past twenty years.

Ted Steinberg, *Acts of God: The Unnatural History of Natural Disasters*. Oxford, England: Oxford University Press, 2000. An environmental historian examines the ten most costly natural disasters in U.S. history. He makes the case that human choices had a lot to do with why they were so devastating.

Periodicals

Neil Baer, "Cardiopulmonary Resuscitation on Television: Exaggerations and Accusations," *New England Journal of Medicine*, June 13, 1996.

Susan J. Diem et al., "Cardiopulmonary Resuscitation on Television: Miracles and Misinformation," *New England Journal of Medicine*, June 13, 1996.

Glen Martin, "The Wings of Life," *San Francisco Chronicle Magazine*, June 1, 2003.

Internet Sources

Air Ambulance Source, "Air Ambulances," September 13, 2003. www.airambulancesource.com/Air-Ambulances.html.

Gary Allen, "Chief Gates Hosts On-Line Talk on Dispatching," *Dispatch Monthly*, 1999. www.dispatchmonthly.com/stories/other/gates_show.html.

American Red Cross, "Disaster FAQs," www.redcross.org/faq/0, 1095,0_378_,00.html.

American Red Cross of Fort Myers, Florida, "National Readiness and Response Corps, Disaster Services Position Descriptions," www.acrossla.org/NRRC/FortMyrsPD.pdf.

J.D. Apgar, "Pennridge Regional Police Department K-9 Unit," June 1998. www.geocities.com/heartland/park/6224/info.html.

Asheville Citizen-Times, "New Emergency Management Degree Program Good Step Toward Protecting Vulnerable Public," January 15, 2003. http://cgi.citizen-times.com/cgi-bin/print/26852.

Neil Baer, "On Call for Hollywood: Harvard Medical School Student Neil Behr on His Experiences as a Writer for the Medical

Drama 'ER,'" *Harvard Focus*, October 1994. http://focus. hms.harvard.edu/1994/Oct7_1994/Students.html.

City of Davis, California, Davis Police Department, "About Us— SWAT," www.city.davis.ca.us/police/AboutUs.cfm?topic=9.

City of Tempe, Arizona, "Ladder Company Operations and History," rev. October 23, 1997. www.tempe.gov/fire/docs/202. 02.html.

Delaware.gov, "Delaware State Police Explosive Ordnance Disposal Unit," June 13, 2003. www.state.de.us/dsp/bomb.htm.

Louis A. Dezelan, "What Do Firefighters Do at a House Fire?" Indianapolis Fire Department, Indianapolis, IN, September 20, 2003. www.indygov.org/ifd/housefire.htm.

Dispatch Monthly, "Communications Center Activities," www. 911dispatch.com/information/act_types.html.

———, "9-Code, 10-Code," www.911dispatch.com/information/ tencode.html.

David Eck, "Career Rescuers in High Demand: 'It's a Good Time to Be a Firefighter,'" *Cincinnati Enquirer*, June 23, 2002. www. enquirer.com/editions/2002/06/23/loc_career_rescuers_in.html.

Federal Emergency Management Agency (FEMA), Emergency Management Institute, Higher Education Project, "Community Emergency Response Teams (CERT)—Frequently Asked Questions," http://training.fema.gov/EMIWeb/CERT/certfaq. asp.

———, "EMI Higher Education Project," http://training.fema. gov/EMIWeb/edu/index.asp.

———, "Select General Emergency Management References," http://training.fema.gov/EMIWeb/edu/highref.asp.

Friendship Fire Department, New Jersey, "Tools of the Trade, Past and Present," www.jersey.net/~dwayne/hist7g.htm.

Monique C. Hite, "The Emergency Manager of the Future— Summary of a Workshop Held June 13, 2003," National Research Council, http://training.fema.gov/EMIWeb/downloads/ HiteMoniquesummary%20.pdf.

Hobson's College View, "Police Officer: To Serve and Protect," www.collegeview.com/career/careersearch/job_profiles/human/po.html.

Imagiverse, "An Interview with Dana Johnson," January 25, 2002. www.imagiverse.org/interviews/danajohnson/dana_johnson_25_01_02.htm.

Sarah James, "Emergency Medical Technician: A Day in the Life," Hobson's College View, www.collegeview.com/career/careersearch/job_profiles/mh/emt02.html.

JobProfiles.org, "Background of a Paramedic," www.jobprofiles.org/heaparamedic.htm.

Susan Kim, "What's a Disaster?" *Disaster News Network*, January 22, 2002. www.disasternews.net/news/news.php?articleid= 1361.

Randall D. Larson, "In the Shadow of September 11th," *9-1-1 Magazine*, www.9-1-1magazine.com/FeatureDetail.asp?Article ID=73.

Life on the Beat.com, "Police Academy—Frequently Asked Questions," http://lifeonthebeat.com/police_academy.htm.

Lifesaving Resources Inc., "Fallen Firefighters, 2001 Statistics," January 10, 2002. www.lifesaving.com/firefighters/stat01.html.

H. Wayne Light, "Distinctive Features of Dispatcher Work," www.911dispatch.com/job_file/distinct_features.html.

Maureen Long, "Just What Is It That Emergency Management Does, Anyway?" International Association of Emergency Manager3, www.iaem.com/EM_Promo_Article_2002.pdf.

Steve Macko, "The Chicago Police Department Bomb Squad," EmergencyNet News Service, January 27, 1996. www.emergency.com/CHBMBSQD.htm.

Beverly Majors, "A Day in the Life: Police Officer Nix's Daily Routine Not a Dog's Life," *OakRidger*, January 20, 2003. www.oakridger.com/stories/012003/new_0120030035.html.

Hillary Mayell, "Women Smokejumpers: Fighting Fires, Stereotypes," *National Geographic News*, August 8, 2003. http://news.

nationalgeographic.com/news/2003/08/0808_030808_smoke jumpers.html.

Ty Mayfield, "2000 JEMS Salary Survey," *Journal of Emergency Medicine*, September 2000. www.jems.com/jms/sept2000/Salary survey00.pdf.

Menlo Park Police Department, Menlo Park, California, "Patrol Ride-Along Program," August 28, 2002. www.geocities.com/menloparkpdtest/ridealong.html.

Ellen Mitchell, "Improving Emergency Responses to Elderly: Efforts Under Way Locally, Nationally," *Newsday*, July 22, 2003. www.newsday.com/news/printedition/health/nyaa3382920jul2 2,0,7634510.story?c oll=ny-discovery-print.

National Law Enforcement Officers Memorial Fund, "Important Dates in Police History," www.nleomf.com/FactsFigures/imp dates.html.

NaturalHazards.org, "Why Should We Be Concerned About Natural Hazards?" www.naturalhazards.org/discover/index.html.

New Jersey Office of Emergency Medical Services, "Choking Adult Instructions for Dispatchers," August 1998. www.state.nj.us/health/ems/adchoke.pdf.

————, "Emergency Medical Dispatch Guidecards," www.state.nj.us/health/ems/guidecard.htm.

New Jersey State Police Office of Emergency Management, "Basic Workshop in Emergency Management, Unit 4: Roles of Government," October 2001. www.state.nj.us/njoem/pdf/wem_4.pdf.

911 dispatch.com, "History of 911," 1995. www.911dispatch.com/911_file/history/911history.html.

Ohio Emergency Management Agency, "Who We Are and What We Do," www.state.oh.us/odps/division/ema/Oema.htm.

Becky Orfinger, "Lessons Learned from the World Trade Center Attack," DisasterRelief.org, November 16, 2001. www.disaster relief.org/Disasters/011115wtclessons.

PBS.org, "Life of a Firefighter," www.pbs.org/testofcourage/life. html.

————, "Test of Courage: Fire Service Statistics," 2000. www.pbs.org/testofcourage/diversity3.html.

PublicSafety.net, "A Detailed History and Story of the Birth of EMS, EMT's, and Paramedics," rev. February 1998. www.publicsafety.net/medic.htm.

RescueHouse.com, "Rules of EMS," www.rescuehouse.com/content/emsjokes/000007.php.

Rebecca Richardson, "Closing the Gender Gap in Emergency Services," Firefighting.com, January 18, 2001. www.firefighting.com/articles/namFullView.asp?namID=1182.

San Antonio Business Journal, "SAC to Offer Emergency Management Degree," November 4, 2002. www.bizjournals.com/san antonio/stories/2002/11/04/daily5.html.

Barbara A. Schwartz, "SWAT Dogs Learn the Ropes," *American Police Beat*, November 13, 2003. www.k9storm.com/news.html.

Christopher T. Shields, "Why I Became a Police Officer," 2000. www.goingfaster.com/tourofduty/why.html.

Spokane Police Department, Spokane, Washington, "Spokane Police SWAT," www.spokanepolice.org/spdswat.htm#deployment.

Daniel M. Telvock, "'It's Not a Boring Desk Job': Every Day Is Different for Police Dispatchers," *Winchester Star*, June 22, 2002. www.winchesterstar.com/TheWinchesterStar/020622/Front_boring.asp.

Karen Thompson, "FEMA Higher Education Project Manager Discusses the New Generation of Emergency Managers," *IAEM Bulletin*, May 2000. www.dola.state.co.us/oem/Publications/prep2001-C.pdf.

————, "The Importance of Investing in a Sound Emergency Management Program," International Association of Emergency Managers, 2002. www.iaem.com/EM_Promo_Article_2002.pdf.

U.S. Department of Homeland Security, Emergencies and Disasters, Response and Recovery, "Fact Sheet: Community Emergency Response Team (CERT) Program," www.dhs.gov/dhs public/display?theme=15&content=835.

U.S. Department of Labor, Bureau of Labor Statistics, *Occupational Outlook Handbook*, 2002–2003. www.bls.gov/oco.

Thomas Wagoner, "A Tribute to Dispatchers," April 25, 2000. www.nd.edu/~dnemeth/ODE.html.

Warwick Police Department, Warwick, Rhode Island, "Special Weapons and Tactics Team/Explosive Ordnance Disposal Unit," www.warwickpd.org/swat.htm.

Women in the Fire Service, "Female Firefighters: A Status Report," 2003. www.wfsi.org/status01.html.

Index

ABC (airway, breathing, and circulation), 25
aerial rescue, 41
aid agencies, 73–74
see also American Red Cross
air transport, for trauma victims, 30, 31
airway, 25
ambulance, emergency medical technician in, 28–29
American Red Cross, 74, 75, 79

back injury, 31–32
brotherhood, feeling of, among firefighters, 44–46

cardiopulmonary resuscitation (CPR), 25–26
civil service system, 13
collapse, of structure, 41
communication
dispatcher and, 11–12, 19, 22
emergency manager and, 74
Community Emergency Response Team (CERT), 85
cross-training, 6

disaster. *See* emergency management
disaster by design, 78
domestic dispute, 57
drugs, administering, 27
duties, of dispatcher, 11–14

elderly, emergencies and, 34

emergency management
focus of, 81–82
mitigation phase of, 76, 78
preparedness phase of, 78–79
recovery phase of, 74, 76
response phase of, 72–74
emergency operations center (EOC), 72–73
emergency response, national to local chain of, 71
emergency response professionals, as working together, 6–7, 57–58
emotional satisfaction
of dispatcher, 15–16
of emergency manager, 82
of emergency medical technician, 29
of firefighter, 46
of police officer, 63
equipment. *See* technology

FBI, 68, 69
Federal Emergency Management Agency (FEMA), 79, 84–85, 86
Web site, 85
firefighters
engine company, 40
truck company, 40, 42
women as, 25, 51, 52
firehouse, life in, 44–46
first contact, emergency dispatcher as, 9, 10–11
first responder

emergency medical technician as, 24
police officer as, 57–58
flight paramedics, 30
future
for dispatcher, 23
for emergency manager, 87–88
for emergency medical technician, 37
for firefighter, 53
for police officer, 69

GEMS (Geriatric Education for Emergency Medical Services), 34

hazardous materials (HazMat) squad, 44
hearing test, 18–19
help, desire to, 8

industrial accident, 43–44
information gathering
by dispatcher, 11–12, 22
by emergency medical technician, 25–26
International Association of Emergency Managers, 85

Jaws of Life, 49
job opportunity
for dispatcher, 21, 23
for emergency manager, 86
for firefighter, 50–51
for police officer, 64, 68–69
job title
emergency dispatcher, 9
emergency manager, 70

K-9 police officer, 66

law enforcement, as a calling, 54
lifesaving skills, 26–27

map-reading skills, 20
medical emergency
dispatcher and, 12
elderly and, 34
military experience, 64
mitigation phase, 76, 78
mobilizing first responders, 12–13
multitasking, by dispatcher, 19–20

National Registry of Emergency Medical Technicians, 27
needle stick, 31–32
night watch, 54
911 reporting system
emergency calls to, 6, 9, 14–15
nonemergency calls to, 16

paramedic programs, 33, 35
planning and disaster preparedness, 78–79
preparedness phase, 78–79
pressure. See stress
public education, 66, 81
recovery phase, 74, 76
rescue company firefighters, 41, 42–44
response phase, 72–74
reward. See emotional satisfaction

risk
for emergency medical technician, 31–32
for firefighter, 46–47
for police officer, 60, 62
role
for dispatcher, 9–11
for emergency manager, 70, 72
for emergency medical technician, 24–26
for firefighter, 39–40
for police officer, 54–57
rules and regulations, for dispatcher, 12

salary
for dispatcher, 21
for emergency manager, 86–87
for emergency medical technician, 35–36
for firefighter, 51, 53
for police officer, 67–68
SCBA (self-contained breathing apparatus), 49
screening and qualifications, for police officer, 63–64
search and rescue company, 41
settings, for work
for dispatcher, 10
for emergency medical technician, 29
for firefighter, 40, 42
for police officer, 58–59
sign-off, 50
skill set
for dispatcher, 18–20
for emergency manager, 82–83

for emergency medical technician, 26–27, 32–33
for firefighter, 47
for police officer, 60
space, confined, rescue in, 41
stress, 7
dispatcher and, 16–18, 23
emergency manager and, 82
emergency medical technician and, 24, 30–32
firefighter and, 47
flight paramedic and, 30
police officer and, 62–63
surveys, by emergency medical technicians, 25–26
SWAT (special weapons and tactics) officer, 61

tactical K-9, 66
technology
for dispatcher, 9–10, 20
for emergency operations center, 72–73
for firefighter, 49
for police officer, 58
for SWAT officer, 61
terrorist attacks, 7–8, 18, 81
training
for disaster response, 79–81
for dispatcher, 20–21
for emergency manager, 83–85
for emergency medical technician, 27, 33, 35
for firefighter, 49–50
for police officer, 64–65, 67
for SWAT officer, 61
typing skills, 20

underground rescue, 41
U.S. Department of
  Homeland Security, 86

vehicle accident, 43
verbal communication
  dispatcher and, 11–12, 19, 22
  emergency manager and, 74
VOAD (Voluntary
  Organizations Active in
  Disaster), 79
volunteer work, 85–86

water rescue, 41
Western Carolina University,
  84
wildland fire, 42
winter/snow rescue, 41
working together, 6–7, 57–58
workload
  for dispatcher, 14–15
  for emergency medical tech-
    nician, 29
  for firefighters, 38–39
  for police officer, 54–57, 59

Picture Credits

About the Author

Tamara Thompson is a professional journalist whose work has appeared in dozens of newspapers, magazines, and Web sites. She is the 2001 update author of *Hidden Tahiti and French Polynesia*, a travel guidebook. She holds BAs in journalism and cultural anthropology from San Jose State University and is currently working on a Master of Social Welfare degree at the University of California at Berkeley. She lives in Oakland, California.